"This book truly is a gift from God through Lisa to all who are trying to find healing from shattered lives. It is of particular benefit to young adults who are searching for a hopeful voice amidst the toxic screeches of the world. Lisa has crafted a beautiful, engaging and provocative story that invites you to look into the heart of a young woman who is struggling to find her way back from great darkness and smothering silence. I cried, laughed and learned from Meri's story. I believe your experiences will be the same."

—*Reverend Dr. Holley Faulkner, Senior Minister, The Baptist Temple, Fairmont, WV*

A heartfelt story about a healing girl. The writing and character development is so effortless I felt like I was experiencing the process with her; seamless and unlike any story in the YA genre at the moment.
—*James Miller, former student and avid reader.*

A timely read for teenagers dealing with happenings of today. This book is an inspiration for young people who may be struggling with a loss. – Kay Prat, retired educator

Well-written, intriguing, and inspiring.
—*Angie Whitlow Wilson, Award winning children's author*

D0423626

Bombs Bursting In Air

Lisa A. McCombs

Publisher Page
an imprint of Headline Books
Terra Alta, WV

Bombs Bursting In Air

by Lisa A. McCombs

©2017 Lisa A. McCombs

All rights reserved. This book is a work of fiction. Names, characters, places and incidents, except where noted otherwise, are products of the author's imagination or are used fictitiously. Any other resemblance to actual people, places, or events is entirely coincidental. No part of this publication may be reproduced or transmitted in any other form or for any means, electronic or mechanical, including photocopy, recording, or any information storage system, without written permission from Publisher Page.

Headline Books, Inc.
P. O. Box 52
Terra Alta, WV 26764
www.headlinebooks.com
Tel: 800-570-5951
Email: mybook@headlinebooks.com

LisaAnnetteMcCombs@yahoo.com

Lisa A. McCombs
358 McCue Avenue
Monongah, WV 26554

Art Director and Cover Design Ashley Teets
www.AshleyTeetsIllustration.com

ISBN 978-1-882658-71-8

Library of Congress Control Number: 2016953096

PRINTED IN THE UNITED STATES OF AMERICA

DEDICATION

This book was written in memory of my personal
war hero, Lance Corporal Michael Pratt.
August 22, 1946-September 14, 2015
Two tours in Viet Nam, US Marine Corps

Thank you to all the men and women who serve
our country.

1

THEATER PEE

If one more bomb sounds, I thought, *my bladder is going to burst.*

"Dad!" Even in my stage whisper, I heard my voice carry throughout the cinema. Dad was engrossed in the action on the screen and obviously mistook my plea as part of the movie script. "Dad, I have to go!"

"Shh!" The hisses from the seats behind us sounded more annoyed than angry, but I still felt guilty. No one liked to waste good money on their entertainment to be interrupted by someone who couldn't keep their mouth shut and their bladder under control.

"You cannot mean it, Meri! You'll miss the best part. Let me check Theater Pee. Can you hold it for a second or two?" Dad quickly tuned into his new phone app that was supposed to advise movie viewers of the appropriate time to leave the viewing area. Mom and I liked to tease him about his obsession with his smart phone but he was probably very excited to try out this new function.

"I can't wait, Dad. Just let me know what I missed."

"Next time don't down an entire 18 ounce Pepsi before the opening credits are over," Dad's admonishing words were accompanied by a chorus of annoyed shushes and disgruntled noises as I climbed over the viewers in an attempt to quietly reach the theatre aisle.

Another loud cinematic explosion made me nearly leap over the last person in the row. I sincerely began to doubt if I would make it to the restroom in time to save myself another reason for embarrassment.

I silently asked myself one more time *why* I had agreed to come to the matinee with Dad today instead of hanging out at the mall with my friends. Since his retirement from the military, he had become even more obsessed with war movies and the need to share these with his family. After three tours in the Middle East, you would think he had enough of war.

I like hanging out with Dad, but we needed to have a conversation about his choice of appropriate entertainment for his teenage daughter. Mom always got out of these outings on the premise of staying home with my baby brother. Since I was their prime babysitter, she knew what my options were. I liked being the big sister, don't get me wrong. Baby Andy is cute, cute, and cute; diaper duty is a BIG drawback, though. Besides, the alternative would have been to watch Holly and Janie try on countless dresses for the upcoming spring dance for which I had no date and was not planning to go.

"I am absolutely pathetic. My life is pathetic. My Saturday is pathetic. My dad's movie choices are pathetic. My social life is pathetic."

"Yea, so join the club."

I had no idea my muttering was actually audible until the voice from the neighboring bathroom stall interrupted my barrage of personal putdowns. I just couldn't seem to keep my mouth shut today.

"Oops. Sorry. I didn't know there was anyone else in here. I hope you're not missing an important scene in your movie."

There was a semi-amused grunt and the sudden flush of the toilet before an answer came.

"As if. If I *ever* agree to come with my sister to another one of these sappy chick flicks…Well, there is no appropriate punishment. Guess I'll just have to invent some ridiculous seven thousand page research paper due in, like, twelve hours when she begs me to come along the next time. I mean, really. We're in college. Does she really think I want to tag along while she mourns the loss of her last douche bag boyfriend by commiserating in the screen presence likes of the most beautiful actresses Hollywood has to offer? I don't see how this helps the situation at all."

I did my own flushing and nearly sighed out loud with physical relief. I did have to congratulate myself on the brilliant idea to consume my entire soft drink so early in the film. This was the second time this month that I had escaped probably the goriest scenes in dad's marathon of blood and guts.

When I exited the stall to wash up, I was surprised that my secret cohort was still in the room. And, she was smoking a cigarette. Or at least, waving a lit cigarette in the air close to the smoke detector. Which obviously was not working.

"I really don't think that's allowed in here," I did my best not to sound judgmental as I lathered my hands with the astringent hand soap.

My eyes met those of the smoker in the mirror just as she tossed the cigarette under the stream of water I intended to rinse.

The girl was about the same age as me, but infinitely more worldly. Her eyes were ringed like a raccoon with the blackest eye liner and her hair was a teased, ratty mass of died black curls. She reminded me of the Wildling character in that HBO series I wasn't supposed to watch. *Of course she is smoking in a public place,* I thought. *That's what her type does.*

Raccoon eyes met my gaze in the mirror, causing me to immediately panic that I had spoken once again out loud. Those thoughts were actually more a reflection of Holly's influence and Janie's attempt to attract the popular crowd than what I really believed; but I also realized shamefully my attitude toward the Goth, EMO, and basically socially inept school crowd was dangerously close to matching my friend's opinion.

I understood the need for social acceptance, but silently was indifferent to appease my gal pals. Life could get a little boring around our small town without the company of a friend or two, so it was my custom to not rock the proverbial boat.

"Well, at least your movie will probably end happily ever after with little to no bloodshed or climate destruction," I checked my teeth in the mirror for popcorn husks and wondered what else I could do to keep away from the big screen.

"Yea, but at least that is reality. I guess you're telling me that you're in the exploding film in Cinema Three? We're right beside you. Daphne, that's my sister, checked her phone to make sure my potty break didn't coincide with any good love scenes."

I had to laugh at that. Evidently the new phone app was a popular item with film goers.

"So, you know that anything you miss will be on instant replay for your viewing pleasure as soon as you leave the theater."

"Yes, but as my sister likes to say, "What doesn't kill us, makes us stronger."

"I think that was Natchez," I hoped I didn't sound as superior as that knowledge made me feel.

"That's who Daphne thinks she is," came her reply and our grins met one another in the reflection.

We joined in a conspiratory giggle as we both reached into our individual pants pockets for identical tubes of Burt's Bees lip gloss.

Tipping our separate glosses in an air salute, we leaned toward the mirror to apply champagne tint to our lips. I had to marvel at the opposite effect of the pale pink lip color. It made me look even younger, but with her wild dyed hair and dramatic eye make-up, she just looked more "out there."

"I'm Americka, by the way. Meri, for short," I said as I rubbed my lips together to even out the thickness of the lip application.

"I bet you have quite the story behind that name. Fiona, here. Nice to meet you, Americka. Why do I feel like I'm about to break out into an old folk song?"

And without prompting, I belted out the first verse of *America the Beautiful* in perfect pitch. Because that's what I do. I sing.

Fiona stood in stunned silence for less than a second before bursting out into laughter.

"That's perfect, Americka. You and that song are as one. Americka, freakin', beautiful!"

I couldn't help it. I started laughing. SO HARD. This would be classified as what Holly called the Stupid Giggles. The perfect stress release, senseless and uncontrollable. But it was nothing compared to what came from Fiona. The tears running down her face turned to black rivers of eye liner as she gulped for air and we nearly fell over one another to sit on the grimy floor and lean against the cold tile of the restroom wall.

"D-do you think that pee-pee app says anything about a laugh break?" I wanted to say something back to Fiona, but when I opened my mouth only a giant hiccup erupted, causing another round of insane laughter.

I don't know how long we squirmed around on that filthy floor, bound together in this shared mirth, neither of us too concerned about movie companions. I couldn't remember the last time I had laughed so hard.

Little did I know this would be the last chance I had to laugh in a long, long time.

We did our best to gain control of ourselves, dry our eyes, reapply the champagne lip goo, and put on our game faces. I checked my watch to affirm that Dad's current war would conclude in less than ten minutes and my arrival would perfectly coincide with the closing credits. Fiona and I shared one last grin and pushed open the heavy restroom door. This hadn't been such a bad day after all.

Until we heard the explosions.

And the screaming.

And realized our lives were about to change.

Forever.

2

END CREDITS

The light. OMG turn off that light! What is going on?
Why is everything so loud? Help me! Dad? Where are you?
Fiona, are you okay? Why don't you answer me?
"Get that one on the gurney!"
"Where's my tourniquet? I need more gauze! Stat!"
"We've got a bleeder!"
WHAT IS GOING ON? Where did all of these people come from? Fiona, where are you?
"Someone get this one on some oxygen!"
"She's not going to make it."
"Bring me that blanket now!"
"Get those children out of here! We've got another ambulance on the way. Just hold on."
Please turn off that light. Where is my dad? What did you do with Fiona? She was right here beside me. Please, somebody answer me!
"Sweetheart, it's okay. Stay with me."
Thank God. Is that you, Fiona? What happened?
"We'll get to your daughter ASAP, Mrs. Bleeker."
"…two more explosions…"
"He had a gun! Why did he have a gun?"
"Is there anyone else in the downstairs theater?"
"There's nothing we can do about that right now. We've evacuated the area. We need to get these people to the hospital RIGHT NOW!"

"Two more cc's of morphine."

Fiona, I can't find my dad. Where's my dad?

"Oh, God, please bring her back to me. I can't lose them both on the same day. I'll do anything…anything…"

My mother's voice woke me and it troubled me that she was crying. I opened my eyes, knowing this had to be a dream. My mother never cried. Not even when Dad was deployed that last time. Not when my baby brother came prematurely and had to stay in an incubator for his first two months on this earth. Not when she lost the last Super Bowl bet with my father and had to take out the garbage (his job) for an entire month. My mother just didn't cry. And she most certainly did not make bargains with God.

So, it had to be a dream.

But, when I opened my eyes, there she was, sitting at my bedside with her head in her hands, pleading with God.

Mom? Mom, it's okay. I'm right here.

She didn't respond and I got scared. *Why wasn't she listening to me?*

And where were we?

This white, bare, cold room was not where I spent most of my days. My bedroom was a virtual splash of color and Bohemian décor. Holly and Janie always made fun of my lack of fashion sense in room decorations, but I loved it. My strobe lights and comfy crocheted Afghans represented comfort. A stark contrast to the perfectly coordinated themes that my friends preferred, my bedroom offered a warmth missing from the obvious planning invested in their rooms.

And there was a stinging disinfectant aroma here that was neither the patchouli of my bedroom nor the Rodeo Drive perfume of theirs. *Mom, what's going on?*

This time when my mother didn't respond to me I desperately stretched my fingers toward her sweater sleeve. Whether it was the movement or that she felt my frightened tug on the material, it brought my mother's attention back to me.

"Oh, Meri! Baby, you're okay. Doctor! She's awake!" Not only does my mother not cry; she doesn't scream. So, this wild screaming woman beside me was not my mother. That was the only conclusion I could fathom.

Mom! Please calm down. I'm fine.

AND, this woman was evidently deaf.

"Nurse! Someone, hurry!" Mom! Stop it. You're scaring me!

The more I tugged at her sleeve, the louder her cries became and the more frantic her plea for help.

Suddenly this sterile, strange room was filled with white clothed individuals, crowding around the bed and pushing my screaming mother out of the way.

"Well, hello, pretty girl. Do you know your name?" An extremely tall, extremely bald, man bent low over my face so that his recent garlic dinner vapored my nostrils in accompaniment with his loud, loud question.

Of course, I know my name. The better question is, what is yours?

"Do you know where you are and why you are here?"

"Oh, please, answer the doctor, Meri!"

Sorry, Mom. I know that was an extremely rude way to answer him. You really did teach me better.

The tall, bald doctor continued to stare intently into my eyes as he shined his very bright flashlight there as well.

"Can you hear me, Meri? My name is Doctor Wells and I am going to be taking care of you for a while. I'm glad to see that you are awake and I hope you're ready to talk with us about what happened to you." Moving beyond his horrible breath, I could tell that he was probably a very caring physician. He just needed to use some mouth wash and turn up his hearing aid.

"Meri, talk to us, baby," Mom had pushed through the mob to my side and was clutching my hand.

I'm right here, Mom. Why can't you hear me?

"Oh, my Lord. She's deaf! Doctor Wells, she can't hear us!"

Of course I can hear you, Mom. It's you that has the hearing problem.

I managed to wrap both of my hands around the one Mom held until she finally got the message that I was indeed communicating with her. I guess the urgency on my face said the words she wasn't hearing.

"Squeeze real tight, baby, if you can hear me."

She didn't say it but I could tell she didn't quite expect the force with which I responded to her request.

"You can hear me? Thank God. Talk to me, then. I need to hear your voice."

I opened my mouth and recited the words that always brought a smile to my parent's eyes. "Oh, beautiful, with spacious skies, and amber waves of grain." At least I thought I said them, tried to sing them, but nothing came out.

It was then that I realized the problem. They weren't deaf. I was, for some reason, mute.

"Oh, no!" My mother turned on a fresh faucet of tears with the realization. "She can't talk! Doctor, she can't talk!"

Sometime after midnight, the hall where I was being kept quieted and I was alone to think. I was still extremely sketchy on what was going on. No one was anxious to share my condition with me and my mother refused to do pretty much anything more than cry and pray to God.

I'm no dummy. There was obviously an enormous tragedy afoot and it concerned my father and me. Since Dad had not been mentioned in my presence I could only assume the worst and that was something I DID NOT want to do.

Being somewhat like my mother, when she was behaving as herself, I rarely panicked...about anything. So, the absence of my voice wasn't really a huge concern. I'm not much of a talker any way and there was no pain, so once again my assumption strategies sprang to work. And I assumed my lack of voice was psychological, not physical. I didn't really care, as long as my vocal chords returned whole and ready to sing.

Throughout high school I have been recognized as THE VOICE. I don't participate in much of anything else extracurricular, but choir and choir is pretty much my life. I love to sing. All Star County Chorus, first chair alto three years in a row and getting prepared for my final go at All State Chorus and the scholarship round next month. Mom and Dad are confident that college funds would be there for me through the military, but I wanted to do this on my own, with my own talents. Earning my way is really important to me and I just feel like that self-fulfillment will make my college years that much sweeter. I know, I know…WAY too mature.

I immediately changed the direction of my thoughts when I habitually opened my mouth to belt out the first two measures of the audition piece I had been practicing.

There was nothing there. No sound. No vibration of vocal chords. No nothing.

Okay, Meri, remember that you do not panic!

I needed a new focus. I looked up at the muted television screen and I saw something that reminded me of Fiona.

At first, even my memory was fogged and I had to think carefully about that name. Fiona. Strange name for a strange girl.

I wondered where she was and hoped she and her sister were okay. Fiona wasn't really the type of person I normally hang out with, but the short time we spent laughing on the bathroom floor had been the most fun I had had in a long while. I guess that's the beauty of sharing time with strangers. They have no preconceived notion of you and you're under no pressure to impress. I wondered where I could find Fiona again.

Just as I was settling into an interesting scenario of a friendship between boring, normal me and my new friend, The Wildling, the picture on the muted television screen switched to a fiery picture of startling destruction. Reporters were huddling around a burning building, dodging emergency vehicles, and vying for air space.

Hey! I know that building!

Struggling to find the TV remote controls that were attached to the bed rails, I activated the volume just in time to hear the news reporter's final words.

"That's all we can report for now. The Ellison Theatre has been declared a total loss. Casualties total fifty-seven at the time of this broadcast and we will share more details as they come clear to us. At this time there is no known information concerning the source of this terrorist attack. We look forward to public comment from the President later this morning. Until then, this is Leitha Myers reporting from channel WWWY, channel 8."

3

NEW AND IMPROVED?

"You don't know how much I appreciate you coming to check on Meri. But, I'm just not certain it's a good time right now."

I could hear my mother's voice outside my hospital room door, but I had no idea who she was talking to. Since seeing the news broadcast and putting together a few pieces of the puzzle, I was aware of the extreme Mother Bear fortress that she had built around this awful, awful room.

She didn't allow visitors. She didn't talk about anyone or anything other than my little brother. She urged me daily, hourly, to speak, and when I showed her the note pad that I was using to communicate, she cried. Again.

I guess I can understand why, since my first written question to her was about Dad. Of course, she didn't answer, but that was okay. I already knew. And I knew the words would only make it real.

From what I could gather, while Fiona and I were afflicted with the Stupid Giggles, three bombs detonated approximately three seconds apart in each of the three cinemas, killing most of the movie viewers and causing the biggest devastation this town has ever witnessed.

If I hadn't gone to the bathroom when I did, I would have been among the dead and/or dying. My scheme to escape the cinematic war that so entranced my dad saved my life; but won him the Purple Medal he so deserved for all of his service to the US Marines. Maybe he had always felt like his time would come in the midst of explosions and warfare. The absence of his comrades was a miniscule detail in those last seconds of his life.

"But, I was there. I was with her when it happened. I really need to see her." A familiar voice was pleading with my mother out in the hallway.

"Maybe another time. When she's home and in familiar surroundings. I just think it's too soon, dear."

Dear? Okay, that was a new one. My non-crying, non-praying, non-panicking mother never used words like "dear." It made her sound so very, very old.

And my mother was anything but old. Janie often commented on the fact that my mother was more like our age than any grown woman she knew. But these last few days had added the age. I could see it in her eyes and in her posture. She wasn't holding up well. It made me sad that I couldn't really be there for her. Although there was nothing really wrong with me other than my frozen vocal chords, as far as I could tell.

"But, Mrs. Miller, I need to see her. We were together when everything happened. I was there. I need to know that she's okay."

And then it hit me. The visitor outside my hospital door was Fiona, the Wildling. And I could only imagine the shock of her appearance on my mother's fragile emotions. If I wasn't so sad, I might have laughed. But I was afraid that might have turned into an uncontrollable bout of hysteria. And that might be terribly painful without the ability to actually let out sound.

In lieu of jumping out of bed and dislodging the assortment of IVs connected to me, I pressed on the Nurse Call button with all my might. That would surely get Mom's attention. I really wanted to see Fiona, weird appearance or not. We had a connection and, like she was telling my mother, she "was there."

The commotion my decision of calling the nurse was a bit over the top. Okay, a lot over the top. My mother's current emotional state was in high anxiety drive and she burst through the door doing that weird panicky thing I wasn't used to.

I raised my hands in the air and tried to calm her down. She skidded (really) to a stop by my bedside and commenced to burst into tears (again).

"Oh, Meri, are you okay? What's wrong, baby?"

I scribbled a few words on my notepad and forced the paper into Mom's hand. I felt the strange compulsion to pat her on the head, similar to what I had seen her do to Andy when he was particularly fussy.

"Why isn't she talking? Americka, what's wrong with your throat?"

The girl asking these questions was a COMPLETE STRANGER and it was my turn to be the inquisitor. Although the voice was familiar, I knew from our brief time together that Fiona would *never* adopt the physical appearance of the girl standing beside my mother. No wonder I hadn't heard Mom shrieking with horror after being approached by this clean cut, socially acceptable individual.

This Fiona was definitely toned down. Her dark hair, not as noticeably hard core black, was slicked back into a neat little pony tail and if she wore eye make-up it was minimal and neutral in color. She was wearing neatly creased blue jeans and a preppy cardigan over what was probably an oxford blouse straight from LL Bean. In her ears were tiny pearl earrings and I swore I caught a glimpse of a class ring wrapped in something fuzzy on her finger.

Now, this girl was definitely more in line with Holly's idea of appropriate. Actually, to the point of nausea.

But there was no denying this was Fiona. Maybe Fiona in drag, but it was her. And the telltale hint of Burt's Bees champagne lip color and faint scent of patchouli oil confirmed that.

What happened to her? A terrorist attack caused me to lose my voice, killed my dad, and totally reconstructed my new friend's appearance?

As my mother fell over her own words in my defense, I quickly scribbled a note and pushed it into her hand.

Mom glanced at it hurriedly and then wiped at her face with the back of her hand.

"Forgive me, er, Fiona? I didn't realize you and Meri were friends before all of this, uh, happened. I don't think we've ever met. How are you? Are you dealing with the aftermath okay? You were with Meri in the middle of all of this? I am so, so sorry." Mom allowed herself a breath before rambling on in confusion. "I'm Mrs. Miller, Meri's mother, of course. This has all been so horrible for her. The trauma has done something terrible to her vocal chords and she cannot talk, but we're confident that it's temporary."

Mom, just stop talking, I silently screamed.

And, amazingly, she did.

My eyes met Fiona's and we shared a small smile in greeting.

"Americka, is it true? You can't talk? You can't sing?" Fiona's words were not pity filled. She just refused to accept the truth. "We can't have that. Americka, you *must* sing."

Interesting this strange girl was so concerned with my singing voice. She had only heard me sing a few lines of my signature song. And that had been under an extreme circumstance of hysteria.

But my singing was obviously of grave importance to her. Until she left my bedside, Fiona was full of suggested exercises to open my vocal chords and put things right with my singing voice. I even detected a small smile tugging at the corner of my mother's mouth as she tried not to laugh at the extreme enthusiasm Fiona put into a couple of demonstrations to make her point.

Fiona didn't stay long, but her visit was certainly uplifting, for my mother as well as for me.

My new friend and I were both thrilled to discover we shared an interest in American Sign Language and that knowledge came in very handy once we realized that ASL was a perfect way to communicate. Mom appeared a bit ill at ease, but she caught on pretty quickly and realized the signing was more for my benefit than for hers. As long as she could interpret the message, there was no need for her to mimic the signs. I wasn't deaf. I just couldn't talk.

Mom seemed a little less sad after Fiona's visit, which lifted some of the increasing emotional pressure I felt. It was when she kissed me good night and went home to be with my little brother that reality began to creep into my brain.

She had to go home to a house once shared with her soul mate, but that now only echoed with his memory. Andy and I were visible reminders (hopefully favorable) of her marriage. She had to look at her home every day, but she would never look at my dad again.

When she looked at Andy she would smile. It was impossible to look at his sweet face and not do so.

But when she looked at me, she would replay the day she received the worst news of her life. And she would wish it was me who was gone and not my dad.

I decided right then that no matter how badly I wanted out of this hospital, I really dreaded going home.

4

GOING HOME

And I was right. Walking through the front door of my home two days later was agony. I heard the theme music from my favorite secret addiction, *The Walking Dead,* rolling through my brain and fervently hoped that a zombie would fall on me from the ceiling and suck out my brain.

The living room was immaculate as always; but now there was a disinfectant odor in the air, not unlike what I had been breathing for the past week in the sterile environment of Regency Central Hospital. But this wasn't a hospital. This was home. And home suddenly had a new personality.

My mom's best friend, Lydia, met us at the door with a finger at her lips to indicate the baby was napping and for us to keep down the volume. No problem here. Unless I just flew into a rage and began throwing things, this girl wasn't making a peep.

Lydia approached me with open arms for her special "auntie" hug, but I avoided the physical contact and squeezed by her on the pretense of putting down my hospital "goodies" (y'know…the plastic pill cup, a packet of tissues, that bed pan that I planned to use as an herb planter) on the floor before tip-toeing up to Andy's room for a peek at my baby brother.

No physical contact. Unless it was Andy, I didn't think I could handle it right now.

Dad was everywhere, but nowhere at all.

Fiona called the house after dinner and asked Mom for my cell number so she could text me. I do not have a cell phone, but all of the sudden I see iPhone in my immediate future. For now, Mom relayed my e-mail address which sent me pronto to my computer screen in anticipation of some conversation.

I was really bummed I had no messages from Holly or Janie, but I suppose I understood their discomfort. I mean, what do you say to someone who has lost her father and her voice within seconds of one another?

Of course, my understanding of compassion was one of the faults for which Holly often chastised me. But it was common sense to me. Someone hurts, you comfort them. Something bad happens to a friend, you give them chocolate.

Well, I didn't have to worry about Fiona's compassion. As soon as I logged on to my Gmail, there she was, surrounded by balloons, teddy bears, Hershey kisses, and candy hearts. Her message looked like a comic book Valentine.

Welcome home! Sorry I didn't get back to the hospital before you left, but we had finals this week. Daphne (my sister) and I had to cram a little to get it all done, but I think we did okay. See what you have to look forward to? But, since you're home and all tucked in comfort, care for a visit? Tomorrow? Afternoon? Clear it with your mother and let me know?

I didn't need to check with my mother. I knew she would be thrilled for me to have a visitor. Especially that sparkly, preppy girl she met at the hospital. But something told me that things were not that simple.

It didn't matter. I was just glad to be home. To sleep in my own bed, in my own room. At least that is what I thought until the bombs began exploding around me in the middle of the night and I woke in a sweat.

I had been on the battlefield with my father at my side. I was terrified, but he was so calm. He had his arm around me and hugged me close to his side amid all the war sounds. He didn't say anything but I knew it was okay. He was okay. It was scary, but in a strange way, comforting.

When I woke I knew he wasn't in the house and that he was no longer on this earth; but I was strangely warm from his touch as if he was trying to tell me something. And I felt better.

As soon as I heard Mom answer the door bell the next day, I knew her tiny shriek was in response to the real Fiona. Mom covered up her reaction well, with an admonishment toward Andy for spilling his sippy cup on the carpet. I'm certain my brother rewarded her with the appropriate infant look of complete innocence and confusion seeing as how he was too young for a sippy cup and his relationship with a carpet was his most recent trick of rolling around on it. Literally one roll per three minutes.

If Fiona was offended I did not hear it in her voice when she greeted my mother. She (Fiona, not my mother) was in the process of offering Mom a plate of something that smelled heavenly when I reached the living room landing.

Our house is a complicated design of layer upon layer, much like a designer tree house. Dad had this weird passion for log-home survival-existence-architecture. When we built the house, he spent many hours playing with Lincoln logs until he had his own unique design set up. Our house was definitely one of a kind and, even though we were not wealthy by any stretch of the imagination, I believe our house could sell for BIG BUCKS based on its unusual layout. Not that Mom would ever consider selling our house. Especially not now.

This house was Dad.

"Fiona, dear, it's lovely to see you again."

There went the "dear" reference again but I could tell Mom was a bit uncomfortable. As any well-meaning, protective mother of young children should be in the presence of an apparent Satan worshipper/Goth/Emo.

"Americka! Look at you, girl! All cozy in your pj's in the middle of the afternoon."

I suddenly felt a bit ill-at-ease. I hadn't even thought about getting dressed. Why bother if I could get away with being a sloth? I wasn't going anywhere.

"That is not at all good for the self-esteem, my girl. Show me to your room and we'll get you presentable."

This coming from Miss Lady of Darkness? The horror on my mother's face was enough to let me know that she was thinking the same thing, but it was also enough to hustle me back up the steps with Fiona hot on my heels.

Even if my vocal chords were in fine tune, they would not have had the opportunity to contribute to the conversation because conversation normally required two or more individuals. Fiona allowed only her own contributions to be voiced. She was a virtual chatterbox while diving (literally) into my walk-in closet in search of suitable attire for a "lady of leisure".

Her chatter was not without interest. Fiona and her identical sister Daphne are freshmen in college and evidently very close. As a defense measure, they began dressing as opposites several years ago when they decided identical twins dressing identically was far too cliché for them. Every morning, when they were in elementary school, their mother found great pleasure dressing them in the same outfit, with the same hair style, and identical accessories. Even their school supplies were the same.

Even though they pretty much shared similar taste in everything, their lack of individuality was rarely an issue for them. By middle school, the sisters realized this lack of difference was not only boring, but rather annoying to people who did not know the difference between them. They were book ends with nothing to show for themselves.

But, they were obviously uniquely different under all of the window dressing, as Fiona called it. She told me her ultimate goal was to become the Tooth Fairy when she grew up. She avidly remembered loosing every single baby tooth and mourning over the fragile little porcelain pieces of herself. So, in twin-like fashion, Daphne is studying to be a dentist. Fiona says she is too scarred by her childhood memories to follow her sister's train of thought. She plans, instead, to go to pharmaceutical school and become an *alchemist*.

Listening to Fiona's narrative was far from boring, but her ramblings ignited some powerful memories for me. As her words entertained herself as well as me, an image of me and my dad flooded my head.

I don't know if it was my first loose tooth, but I remember one barely hanging to the point where it was flopping around in my mouth.

I remember tagging it with my tongue, but dared not do anything more aggressive.

It was movie night. That seemed to be what my dad and I did most together. Mom had a book club meeting and Dad and I had a date to snuggle up on the sofa and watch the annual TV broadcast of *The Wizard of Oz*. He promised me the experience of a lifetime. Complete with homemade buttered popcorn.

Evidently, it was an American movie ritual to play this movie annually on this particular day and history was being made with this, the last annual, nationwide viewing of the great wizard.

As always, I was thrilled to spend private time with Dad. I was his princess. No one could make me feel more important.

When I refused his offer of husk-free popcorn, Dad demanded I show him my dangling tooth. I'm sure it was caked in dried blood and pretty gross looking.

On the first commercial break, he collected his "tools" and prepped me for my first test of bravery of the evening. (The second test had to do with monkey's flying around a witch's house, but I remember being more afraid of the wind storm that swept up Dorothy and Toto than those silly looking monkeys. I mean, really. Flying monkeys?) And when Dad gently wrapped one end of a piece of string around my tooth and attached the other end to the handle on the front door, I remember kind of panicking.

But his plan didn't provide the satisfaction (entertainment) he had hoped, because my tooth fell out as soon as the weight of the string pulled it loose from its roots. My first memory of being promised a visit from the mysterious Tooth Fairy was made.

I looked at Fiona now and nearly fell off my bed in silent laugher.

Most children saw the Tooth Fairy floating on a cloud of gauze and tulle. Fiona's midnight eye liner and spiked hair did not play into the average child's imagination.

"What? You don't think green is this season's go-to color?"

Fiona was holding up a new spring sweater I hadn't worn yet. In fact, I spied the price tag still attached to the sleeve. While I took a walk down Memory Lane, she had been rooting through my closet for the appropriate fashion statement for today.

Of course, this irony incited in me more laughter and with the absence of sound, my body reacted by compensating with a stream of tears that initially alarmed my guest. Fortunately her ability to "read" my muteness created the perfect occasion for a round of Stupid Giggles of which Holly would be proud.

Fiona had no idea what we were laughing about. She played along for the joy of laughter. In actuality, I really didn't know why I was laughing either, but it felt good.

My mother, bless her, treated Fiona and I to a special lunch of vegetarian chili (Fiona was not a vegetarian, she informed me in sign language when Mom's back was turned. Neither were we, so this menu item was a little mysterious) and with the help of Lydia we had an official Ladies Who Lunch afternoon.

It was good to see Mom trying to be not so sad, but as soon as our guests were gone, the empty air apace was consumed with echoes of who was missing.

My dad.

5

More Than A Church Thing

Children who suffer from Selective Mutism speak in at least one setting and are rarely mute in all settings. Most have inhibited temperaments and manifest social anxiety. For children with Selective Mutism, their mutism is a means of avoiding the anxious feelings elicited by expectations and social encounters. Children with traumatic mutism usually develop mutism suddenly in all situations. An example would be a child who witnesses the death of a grandparent or other traumatic event.

To fill up the emptiness after Mom put Andy to bed later that evening, I organized myself at Dad's computer in the little room beside the kitchen. Mom and I had teased him about not wanting to use the actual office space at the back of the house in case he missed getting to taste-test any of the ongoing new recipes Mom played with in an attempt to broaden our dining experience.

After sitting in his orthopedically designed computer chair, I realized that was only part of his attraction to this location. It was close to the heart of our home. There was always someone in the kitchen. This was not a lonely place.

So, my father's computer (He called it Ralph for some weird reason) told me more about my condition. Evidently this was not a permanent situation and I guess I had some control over it. Evidently it is an anxiety issue and I certainly understood how one can become anxious after being involved in a "terrorist" attack, even if it wasn't as world shattering as 9-11.

Death is death. Pain is pain.

Mom has tried her best to shield me from news surrounding what occurred at the theater that day, but she underestimated my need to know. And the internet has provided me enough information to piece together a newsworthy story.

And this is what I have: A group of students at our local college planned this event as a sort of "practice" run for a bigger attack they hoped to initiate in the closest major city to us. They were working under the guidance of their (misguided) political beliefs to provide a public statement to sway Americans to understand our (supposedly) misguided way of life. In other words, these college students have been brainwashed to believe that our country's belief system is false.

Of course, my question is, *What could be wrong with a desire to live in a peaceful country?* We may have our differences and there may be times of discontent, but the premise is consistent.

As my namesake song promotes, we are the "land of the free and the home of the brave." What's wrong with that?

According to a local news article, the accused were not only unfortunate (for them) to be caught, they will stand trial for premeditated murder of innocent citizens and a decorated war hero who survived three military tours of their very country in an attempt to bring peace to their troubled lands.

Talk about misguided appreciation.

The fact that society is angry about this event doesn't bring my dad back, though. From what I have read, most terrorist attacks are a result of anger. Anger solves nothing.

And the more I thought about it, the more anger I felt rising to the surface. This was definitely counterproductive,

I needed to work on a more positive attitude for Dad's upcoming memorial service, being planned by Lydia since my mother appears to be working perfectly through the stages of grief and is currently stuck on the denial phase.

Not being church people, we do not have a minister to perform the service and Mom doesn't want it to be all military—even if his military associations were Dad's only surviving extended family. I think sometimes Mom felt like the other woman.

When Fiona caught wind of our theological predicament she offered her own assistance and insisted I attend church with her on Sunday, and that's tomorrow. I promised her I would enlist her fashion sense in assembling the appropriate church outfit.

I logged off of Ralph and headed to my room. Tomorrow I planned to remove Ralph to my room in exchange for my little laptop. Mom couldn't even glance in the direction of Dad's off-kitchen office. She rarely used the computer anyway. So, Ralph's absence probably wouldn't even register with her.

I turned off all the lights in the kitchen and living room since Mom evidently was already tucked away in her own room. Her bedroom door used to be always open and inviting, but is now tightly sealed shut against any more anguish. She had taken to sleeping with Andy in her bed and I wanted to be snuggled in the mix there.

Something told me to walk on by, though. The temptation was strong, but there was something I had to do.

I needed to find something to wear to church. Since Fiona was my only role model…Of course, selecting the correct Fiona identity to emulate was a challenge.

Rooting through my closet, now neatly ordered after Fiona's recent search, I found a wool skirt that I didn't remember ever wearing, a denim jumper a bit frayed at the hem, and a pair of black leggings that I like to top off with my favorite oversized turtle neck sweater.

She told me that her church was rather casual and that the congregation did not abide by the stereotypical dress code of days gone by. (She actually said that. "Days gone by." When my voice returns, I think I want to speak like Fiona.)

An overwhelming yawn reminded me that it was long after my bedtime, so, I opted for the comfort of my favorite outfit; arranging it carefully over the back of my desk chair before turning out the light and closing my eyes.

I lay there for several seconds, waiting for someone to wish me sweet dreams, but there was only silence. Not even a murmur from Mom's room down the hall.

Sometimes going to bed is so anticlimactic.

But then, Dad came to visit again. This time we were not in a war zone exactly. And he didn't seem to know I was with him. In fact, it was as if I was floating on the ceiling watching him.

He sat in a worn easy chair in a strange room. He was all alone amid the messy clutter of empty pizza boxes and discarded soda cans. I thought that was strange because my dad was such a neat freak. After several attempts to catch his attention I decided to explore instead.

The room held three twin-sized beds and two large desks. There were books stacked everywhere and clothes piled in every corner. Definitely a guy's room, I thought.

When I spotted a varsity jacket hanging on a nail on the wall I knew where we were. This had to be Dad's college dormitory room. I looked back over at my father and realized something I hadn't caught earlier. He was much younger and even sported the beginnings of a beard. A beard and my father did not make sense. He was always clean shaven, military polished. I was seeing my father before he knew me or possibly before he even knew I would ever exist.

I didn't know much about his college days or the time before he and my mother married, so this was like opening a new chapter in the life of Rick Miller. I was kind of excited at this discovery until I heard the soft sounds of weeping.

My dad was never afraid to share his feelings, but he was a proud man and did his best to keep his private thoughts to himself. Yet here he was all alone in this dingy room, wrapped in some unseen grief.

I wanted to comfort him like I remember him comforting me so many times, but he slipped right through my arms. In fact he was beginning to fade from my sight and I tried to cry out to him, but I had no voice. He wouldn't have heard me anyway. Somewhere in my dream I knew this was a dream. I just wanted him to hear me.

In the brief seconds before the dream dissolved into that magical fairy dust of awakening, I got a glimpse of the open book my dad held on his lap. It was a beautiful book with fragile pages rimmed in gold leaf. I had never seen this book before, but it looked old and very, very important.

I left my dad in his grief, but I didn't feel sad. Just confused.

The next morning I discovered my outfit selection was spot on and Fiona was actually dressed very similarly. Or maybe it was Daphne. Since I had yet to meet Fiona's bookend, I wasn't sure, until I was enveloped in loving arms and knew this twin was the one I knew.

Based on their names, I had kind of expected parents of a throw-back sixties era, still traumatized by Vietnam. But Fiona's mom and dad couldn't look more normal, stable, and well-adjusted. And happy. Not a giddy, over-the-top happy, but a sincerely genuine content-ment. They touched one another often and smiled tenderly at their daughter with respect as well as parental adoration.

Their welcome expressions when Fiona introduced me were real. They expressed their sorrow for my loss but did not dwell on it. Their attitude seemed to say they really were very sorry, but life often dealt a bad hand.

No one mentioned or explained Daphne's absence and when she had not appeared by the time the service began, I was more than curious.

Even though Fiona assured me her church was very much laidback, Reverend Hawkins' brand of preacher-image really put me in tizzy. He was a member of a motorcycle group called Bikers for Christ and his otherwise preppy attire of khaki jeans and button down shirt was strangely enhanced by a worn black leather jacket that held a large family of badges and pins. He wore his black hair long and pulled into a low ponytail. I remembered my dream Dad's unshaven appearance and wondered what he would think about this unmilitary grooming. I found it rather comforting and very Jesus-like. For as much as I knew about Jesus, that is.

The reason for Fiona's "normal" attire was for church. She told me in a hushed voice she and Daphne appeased their parents on Sundays by being what they are—identical twins. I looked forward to meeting Fiona's alter ego.

The church experience was nothing like I could imagine. When the music started, bringing everyone to their feet, I felt something special happening right in the center of me. There was nothing pious or quiet about what came from the singers on stage. And any concept of reverence flew out the window when the handsome Reverend Hawkins opened his mouth and released the first measures of his prayer in song.

He could truly be a rock star. I wondered if he had ever auditioned for one of those television talent shows that were so popular. Holly would be all over this. He was just that good.

We stood for nearly twenty minutes as the congregation joined in what Fiona referred to as the praise band in worship, from one song into the next. It was beautiful and even though I was not familiar with the lyrics to the songs, my love for music allowed me to hear the harmony in my mind. So, I too, participated in my own fashion.

If the minister hadn't asked us to be seated when he did, I believe the congregation could have continued singing for the entire service. It was so powerful. When my behind met the velvety cushion of the church pew, I felt as if I had just completed a cross country event rather than the beginning of a spiritual service. I was wiped out.

But when Reverend Hawkins began to speak I became mesmerized for an entirely different reason.

Much of what he said didn't make a lot of sense to me, but I understood the general message and appreciated the interesting interpretation of some very heavy reading material. If I didn't know he was a real life preacher, I might have been searching the sky for lightning bolts.

Reverend Hawkins was truly one of a kind and I wasn't exactly sure how to take his whole James-Dean-Rebel- Without-a-Cause (thanks to Dad's addiction to movies of all kinds) religious attitude. He talked about Jesus being a renegade and a trouble maker.

When Fiona pointed out the list of suggested scripture to read this week, I got really excited about accepting the challenge. I just had to find a Bible somewhere in our house. Every house has a Bible, doesn't it? Funny I never thought about it before, but my family's church time consisted of the requisite Christmas and Easter showing.

After church, Fiona's family insisted I join them for their Sunday tradition of dinner at a local restaurant, but I felt guilty leaving Mom at home alone and signed to Fiona I should probably go home.

"Did you enjoy yourself, Meri? I actually heard you humming at one point. That's cool. Pastor Hawkins is always on the lookout for new talent. Maybe you'd be interested in joining the Praise Team? I mean, if you would like to come with me again?" I found my head bobbing up and down with an energy that was frightening. Yes, I wanted to go back there again. In fact, I didn't really want to leave right now.

"Oh, and don't forget to have your mother call Pastor Hawkins about, y'know. He was a Marine, too." Fiona parked her little yellow Volkswagen Beetle in my driveway before reaching across the gear shift to surprise me with a hug. "Thanks for coming, Meri. Here's a copy of the church bulletin and that list of scripture. After you read some, if you want to talk about it, just e-mail me. I should have some free time this week. Daphne has decided she wants to work all of our shifts at the book store this week. I guess there's a cute new guy who has been stopping by everyday around lunch time and she is convinced he's checking her out."

I tried to share Fiona's amusement but only managed a silly grin. So, that's why Daphne wasn't in church today. These twins really had no reason to fear not being individuals. They were obviously much different than people would ever know.

"A Bible? Do we have a Bible?" My mother didn't try to hide her exasperation at all. "So, you go to church one time with your new friend and you are a Bible Thumper?"

Mom's reaction to my question was surprising. I told myself to research the stages of grief again. She seemed to be progressing at an unusual rate. Or maybe I was mixed up on the order. Did anger come before or after denial?

I wished more than anything my voice would cooperate because I really wanted to discuss my church experience with Mom. In the past, it was Dad with whom I shared most thoughts, but I wanted Mom to know what a great time I had this morning. I really believed it would make her feel a little better to hear about Pastor Hawkins and the casual feel of Fiona's church.

Besides, what was a Bible Thumper? The connotation of that reference was nothing like the pure joy I felt while at Fiona's church.

"Oh, by the way, Holly called while you were out and when I told her you were still not talking, she said to be sure to check your e-mail." While she spoke to me, Mom opened and closed half a dozen drawers in the dining room hutch until she finally slid a worn leather covered volume across the table toward me. Without sparing a glance at the book, she continued talking.

"I'm a little concerned about you being so buddy-buddy with someone Fiona's age, Meri. You need to reconnect with Holly and your school pals. And I think you should go back to school next week. Being back in familiar surroundings should help you get over this vocal trauma."

The cover of the imposing book in front of me was a glossy dark-blue leather. Worn in places, this Bible obviously had some road time. It wasn't new. The words *Holy Bible* were engraved into the soft book binding. Underneath that in skillful calligraphy was my father's name.

Mom, Holly hasn't even been here to visit. Is that the kind of friend you really want me to have?

I looked up at my mother who was still rambling on about the importance of friendships and appropriate age groups. I shrugged, unnoticed, and continued to inspect this treasure in front of me. There was something hauntingly familiar about this book, but I shook off the creepy feeling and tried to tune in to my mother again.

"So, once you get back to school and we put all of this ugliness behind us, life should settle down. You'll see. You won't want to be around those strangers any longer."

But Fiona isn't a stranger. We have something very important in common. We survived something really, really horrible.

Carefully, I opened the front cover of the Bible. In faded ink I found my father's name printed in his careful penmanship. The writing held a strong resemblance to the rank and file of a military squadron. The pages were of a silky onion skin material and the edges were etched in gold leaf.

That's Dad. Always the precision machine.

So, somewhere along the way Dad had a relationship with God or had participated in a church family.

"So, make sure you get in touch with Holly, Meri. I'm sure she's really worried about you."

Yeah, right.

Mom finished wiping at the immaculate kitchen counter and almost shyly moved her eyes to my face. She hadn't really looked at me for a while, always teasing the edge of my existence.

"Just don't forget, Meri, how much I love you. This is a really, really bad thing we're going through and I am so proud of you for holding up so well. We just need to have patience with one another. We'll get through this."

I hugged my mother and silently excused myself to take Dad's Bible to my room.

6

SANCTUARY

I spent most of Monday and Tuesday poring over the pages of ancient times and not really understanding most of it. When I e-mailed Fiona with my dilemma, she told me to stay away from the wordy book of Exodus and look at Proverbs or the New Testament. This made for more enjoyable reading, but it also reinforced the need to understand the *why* of what I was reading. I promised to meet her at the church tomorrow evening for a youth Bible study class if Mom agreed.

The memorial service for my dad will begin at 10:00 a.m. and I dread the military aspect more than anything. That lone bugle player on the hill above the National Cemetery where all good soldiers are buried would make everything final. It promised to be a super emotionally-charged day and I really couldn't begin to predict the level of anxiety and grief that would surely fill our home after the service.

Mom was still going through the motions, but Lydia was actually the one making arrangements and organizing plans. Mom had given Lydia the green light on the service program and when I suggested contacting Pastor Hawkins she gratefully agreed. I think Dad would approve of the rebellious side of this man of the cloth.

Lydia had arranged for a quiet reception at our house following the service and, knowing my father's friends, this would be anything but quiet. I just hope it doesn't upset my mother too awfully much. I'm glad Andy is far too young to understand what is going on. I had at least a few years to know our father.

In the meantime, I contacted Holly and Janie to inform them of the funeral arrangements and let them know I would return to school on Friday. Janie did not return my e-mail. Holly sent her regrets. She wouldn't make it to the memorial service since "funerals were just so depressing."

No, shit, Sherlock.

And Mom wanted me to stay loyal to this "friend"?

But I could not stay bitter.

Proverbs 17:17 says that "a friend loves at all times" and whether I attend church regularly or not, that just makes sense. So, I have to forgive Holly for being so shallow and I have to respect her honesty. Sure, no one wants to willingly attend a funeral and be all sad. This isn't her sorrow to experience. It's mine. And no matter what, she will still be my friend and I will be hers.

I guess.

"Then I saw an angel standing in the sun. He shouted in a loud voice to all the birds in mid-air: 'Come and gather together for God's great feast!' "

Pastor Hawkins' choice of sermon topic could not have been more perfect for a military funeral. He spoke of generals and armies, false prophets and avenging angels, and food. Lots and lots of food; for the soul, as well as for the stomach.

Mom and I held hands throughout the entire service and when the bugler took his post to play taps, the tears fell freely from all present. Because there was no burial, there was not a grave to mourn over and Mom didn't wish to hang around the mortuary any longer than necessary. So we piled in the car with Lydia and headed back to the house, where Fiona's mother greeted guests and performed the perfect hostess responsibilities.

I don't know why she was there, but Lydia must have hooked up with her. Fiona worked the corners of the living room. There was soft instrumental music playing from an iPod set up beside Dad's giant flat screen television that no one ever watched.

I could smell the comforting aroma of spicy meatballs and garlic bread emanating from the kitchen. Delicate plates of cookies were strategically placed on end tables and book shelves. There were bottles of soft drinks and water in a large ice bucket that I had never seen before on the kitchen island.

If it wasn't such a somber occasion, the entire atmosphere could be mistaken for a party or celebration. As if reading my mind, Fiona hooked her arm into my own and squeezed me slightly. "We're here to celebrate the life of your father, Meri. He had to have been a great man because he has such a wonderful daughter."

Mom did her best to keep it together for her guests, but her presence didn't last long before she made excuses to tend to Andy upstairs, never to reappear for the rest of the day.

Dad's military friends gathered around her before she left the room and then said their goodbyes with a small salute in my direction.

And then…it was over. I don't know how long I stood in the middle of the empty living room, but Fiona's soft words startled me into consciousness.

"That was beautiful, Meri. Have you tried opening your mouth and really letting it out?"

I had no idea what she was talking about until Lydia put her arms around me in a tight hug.

"Oh, Meri, baby. Your voice is back. Let's go tell your mother!"

Before Lydia could pull me up the stairs to announce the miracle to Mom, I shook my head fiercely and pulled out of her grasp.

"I wish Daph had heard that. The two of you would make an awesome duet," Fiona murmured.

Maybe I had been singing, or humming, or something. But I wasn't ready to announce to the world that my voice was back. I opened my mouth to convey this to the others in the room, but when I tried, my voice was still silent. The only sound I made was a tiny vibration of defeat.

7

THE POSTER

"I know how it feels to be disappointed in friends, Meri. And I've learned those folks weren't really true friends to begin with. They were with you as a matter of convenience or status or something equally as trivial. Don't worry about their lack of support for you right now. They just need some time to mature."

I listened to Fiona chatter on, really listening to her words and not being offended by what she was saying. If I had learned anything about Fiona it was that she was not judgmental. If Holly, or even Janie when she was thinking for herself, was here she would insist Fiona was pointing a finger in her direction

That was silly, of course. Fiona had no ulterior motive nor need to override my relationship with my friends. If that *is* what they are.

Holly and I had been gal pals since first grade. We did everything together. But then Janie moved to town and Holly's devotion was split. She had me, the constant, who listened to her boy woes and complaints about her parents with a silent lip and a compassionate nod. But Janie was someone new to mold into her lackey. I had known that for a long, long time, but never had the motivation to pull Janie out of the quicksand of Holly's influence.

No matter what, though, I believed Holly would always be my friend. But, today she had failed a true test of that friendship.

Aunt Lydia nearly jumped up and down when I asked her to take me to the mall to meet Holly. I don't know why everyone was so concerned about my social life lately. It wasn't as if I locked myself in the dark confines of my bedroom when I wasn't in school. I did my school work, played with Andy, helped Mom with the house-work, and attended church with Fiona. That seemed like a fairly full schedule for a teenager.

But when Holly texted me to meet her at the mall for an afternoon of just the two of us, Mom and Aunt Lydia behaved as if I was going to the prom or something. And their enthusiasm got me excited. It was going to be just like old times. Me and Holly doing me and Holly things.

We were to meet at Starbucks at 11:00. By 11:30, I was getting antsy. By 12:00. I was worried. And when Holly had still not materialized by quarter after the lunch hour, I broke down and texted her on my new cell phone.

Fiona walked by my table-for-two as I finished my second Grande latte and read the belated reply from Holly. She wasn't coming. In fact, she and Janie were actually on a bus to Pittsburgh for a day of shopping at the BIG MALL. They had it planned for days. She didn't even apologize for standing me up or forgetting about our date, whichever the case might be.

"I'm not going to tell you to make excuses for her, Meri. This is just plain rude. But maybe, just maybe, she really did mark the events down wrong on her social planner. We must always give others the benefit of the doubt."

I appreciated Fiona's words and the fact she wanted to keep Holly in a good light; but my heart just wasn't in the forgiveness mode at the moment.

"So, how many of those caffeine bombs have you had? How about some *real* lunch?"

Before I could protest, Fiona had me by the hand and was marching me down the mall to the food court, chattering all the way. We settled for a greasy meal of fish and chips that I knew I would pay for later, but I relished in the extravagance for now. I would just double up on the acne cream later tonight.

Fiona had just announced she would drive me home and there was no reason to bother Aunt Lydia, when she saw the poster.

"Meri! Look at this! This is perfect. You must sign up!"

I stared, horrified, at the announcement for an upcoming talent show to be staged right here in the very location that housed the sign. "This is a fantastic opportunity, Meri! I bet if you open up that mouth of yours and sing, you will be talking in no time."

I scanned the details of the event and cringed. Was she serious?

"I've been trying to convince Daphne to do something like this forever. Too bad I can't get you two together to sing a duet."

The tone of Fiona's voice was suddenly mournful and a wave of concern shot up my spine. Why couldn't she get us together? Even though I had yet to meet Fiona's twin, the idea of sharing the stage was a lot more appealing than going solo.

Before I could find my note pad and question her, Fiona was her bubbly self, babbling about song choices and a new dress.

"What about "Hallelujah" by Leonard Cohen? Better yet, you should do an updated version of a classic hymn. Daphne's fave is "Amazing Grace." Oh, Meri, this is going to be so awesome. Just what we need."

Just what *we* need? What was she talking about? If Fiona wanted to be on stage so badly maybe *she* should sign up for the show.

Before she could get too far ahead of me (as if she weren't already) I grabbed the sleeve of her sweater and pointed emphatically at my note pad.

But, I can't sing!

"Don't be silly, Meri. You can do anything you want to do. You are Americka the beautiful, the talented, the amazing. You rose from the flames just like that Hunger Games chick. There is a reason why you survived that explosion." Tears were rolling down Fiona's cheeks, creating an ebony river of mascara and eye liner. "And that reason is for you to sing. Sing to the angels, Meri. Sing for your dad."

Fiona swiped at her drippy nose with her sleeve. "You have a purpose. You *can* sing and you *will* sing. You *must* sing for those who cannot."

Later that the evening I remembered her use of the plural "we" in referring to "my" singing experience. I really hadn't given Fiona's emotions much thought since the bombing. She was always so *up*. So on top of everything.

Today, though, showed me that even if she did not lose her voice, any body part, or her father, the bombing was still affecting her. Neither of us had emerged from "the flames" unscathed.

Maybe I *could* sing for Fiona. She seemed to have all the confidence in the world in me. I plugged in my new computer headphones and slipped in the CD of mixed praise tunes Fiona dug out of her Volkswagen glove compartment. The least I could do was listen to a few songs.

8

BACK IN THE SADDLE AGAIN

Not much had changed in the halls of Ellison High. But that seemed to be the way with personal tragedy. Life doesn't change much for those who are not affected.

I fought my way through the pushing and shoving of testosterone youth to find my locker decorated with a helium balloon and a collage of cutesy sympathy cards I assumed were from Holly and Janie. I really didn't want to deal with their sympathy, though. My goal was to get through the day as normally as possible.

I promised Fiona I would make time to visit one of the school's private music rooms to listen to her song choice for the talent show. Even though I knew in my heart I would disappoint her, I could at least enjoy the quiet atmosphere of the sound proof cubicle.

And by the time my lunch hour arrived I was ready for a little private time.

Holly was her usual "look at me" self while she acted as my self-appointed translator and body guard. Even if I could talk for myself, I do not think she would have allowed it. Her act of overly concern actually made me feel worse than I already did. When she saw my bagged lunch there was no end to her exaggerated sighs of disapproval. Because, she reminded me, "Only losers bring cold lunch to school."

By the time the lunch hour arrived I couldn't wait to take my bagged tuna sandwich and bypass the cafeteria to be a loser in practice room 3.

For a second I contemplated the significance of the room number. Room number 3. Three bombs detonated in three separate cinemas, three seconds apart.

"Enough, Americka!" Whether I actually spoke the words or just yelled loudly at my inner self, I didn't know. It wasn't really important, was it?

At first I wasn't certain what do to. I looked at myself in the floor-to-ceiling mirrored wall to see if I had grown a second head or if the word g-r-i-e-f was written across my forehead. The way teachers had avoided eye contact all morning and Holly's persistent attention made me wonder if maybe there was something physically apparent about my horrible experience.

I got face-to-face with the mirrored wall and gazed into my own eyes until my eyeballs crossed.

Suddenly I was possessed with a strong urge to laugh. And I mean really laugh. That guttural, belly laugh that bordered on hysteria. It started in my chest and I could feel it branch out into my stomach region before it actually rose to my throat. And then, there it was. I was laughing. Out loud.

The sound of my own laughter was startling at first and then the physical effect took over. The room was sound proof, so there was no fear of being overheard. And this felt good, so good. I allowed myself to roll on the carpeted floor, hugging my arms around my belly and pounding my open palms soundlessly on the ground.

When I heard the distant peal of the fifth period bell, I couldn't believe I had spent thirty minutes simply laughing.

I checked my appearance in the wall mirrors and was alarmed by the dried river of mascara on my cheeks and the ratty mess of my normally well-groomed hair. I guess my lunch activity had involved a little hair tearing.

When I felt the hysteria rise once again in the back of my throat, I quickly broke eye contact with my mirrored image and gathered my things.

I pulled my hair back into a neater pony tail and wiped my hands across my face in an attempt to erase any evidence of a cosmetic mishap before tossing my lunch bag in the trash and allowing myself a final glimpse at my reflection.

I was still the same Meri. Just a little crazed, but the same person.

I guess this is what some folks refer to as therapy.

Even though I felt guilty for not listening to Fiona's CD, I felt better about being back in the saddle of school. And I was excited to have a private place to go when things got weird.

Looked like Room 3 and I were going to spend a lot of time together in the future.

9

So, What Do You Think?

If I felt guilty earlier about not listening to Fiona's CD, that guilt multiplied two fold when I checked my e-mails prior to going to bed that night. Fiona must have had a very light schedule today by the look of my inbox.

She cornered the market on the number of times and ways one could inquire on someone's opinion. Basically it boiled down to what I thought about her CD recording of Daphne's favorite hymn. Not proficient at lying, I really didn't want to begin now. Talk about that guilt factor!

If anyone would understand my practice room incident it would be Fiona, but something told me not to treat the situation lightly. She really had a vested interest in this talent show, even if I was not at all confident that it was something within my ability. And she was truly the only friend I seemed to have.

So, I dug out my headphones and plugged myself into Fiona's world. If nothing else, her CD should provide a relaxing atmosphere for sleep.

When sleep had not visited by midnight, I could not blame my open eyes on insomnia. It amazed me the variety of ways one song could be performed. And I think Fiona had covered them all. The singing voice was the same for all the recorded renditions, and I could only assume that the artist was Daphne. More than once a beautiful harmony emerged and I wondered if that second voice was Fiona. The intonation was too similar not to be.

Never having met Daphne, I had no basis for comparison, but I made a mental note to remedy that very soon. The girl couldn't be *so* busy that she couldn't manage a brief introduction. Could she? If the twins were basically inseparable, there had to be a time when I could meet Fiona's twin.

I didn't know what the problem was.

But I did know Fiona's chosen performance song was *amazing*, no matter which arrangement was presented. I could only assume the song writer knew that would be the perfect descriptor assigned to the song when he or she penned it. "Amazing Grace" could not be described as anything else but amazing.

Hoping Fiona was not on line at this late hour because I really needed to get to bed, but not wanting to risk losing the excitement I felt at that moment, I sent her an e-mail confirming the perfect song choice. I sent the message and quickly shut down my computer before she had a chance to reply. The elation the song had inspired in me made me know that if Fiona replied immediately I would be up the rest of the night chatting on line.

Even with my very mature decision to seek sleep before the morning light, I could not get the song out of my mind or the haunting words out of my ear.

"I once was blind, but now I see…" I wondered if I could turn that around to "I once was mute, but now I speak."

In an attempt to "put the issue to bed" I remembered a tactic my dad taught me several years ago. He had a collection of colorful post-it notes that were often visibly stuck to items on his computer desk. They were reminders, lists, and phone numbers. When the hour got late or the deadline got closer, Dad would tell me those items became his priority list. He said to write them down and know that I could deal with them first thing the next day.

I picked up my favorite neon green pack of post it notes and wrote down two priorities for tomorrow, I mean today.

1. Meet Daphne.
2. Take "Amazing Grace" to practice room
3. With that accomplished, I turned down my bed covers and climbed in with a satisfied mind.

My dad-dream was even less confusing and simple in its message. As I drifted off into never, never land, I felt the touch of my Dad's lips caress my forehead in a tender kiss good night.

10

PRACTICE ROOM 3

My hands were trembling and I even broke out into a little sheen of perspiration as I stared at the reflection of me that stared back from the music room wall. With the intro to "Amazing Grace" emanating from the sound system, I dared that reflection to join the instrumentals with the first words of the first verse. I didn't care if I was of pitch (an issue I would never have admitted in the past). I just wanted to hear some sound. My sound.

My entrance came and went and I couldn't even open my mouth, let alone force air up and out of that orifice. This was going to be a long session. I could feel the hot tears flooding my eyes and I angrily wiped them away. This was not the road to progress. Tears were not allowed.

I paused the music and took a deep breath. I had no witnesses to my failure. No pressure here but what I inflicted upon myself. If this muteness was selective, I selected this moment to be the perfect opportunity to overcome my affliction. No one had to know but me and that mocking reflection in the mirror.

And then it hit me. I did have a witness and she was winning the stare-down contest at the moment. I could not allow this to happen.

Quickly breaking eye contact with myself, I turned to face the opposite wall and took another deep, deep breath. In one of her many soliloquies, Fiona had rattled on about meditation and the healing yoga she and Daphne like to practice. She really believed we had to find peace from deep within ourselves before sharing that peace with the world. I had to shut out the rest of the world and be at one with myself.

As the opening measures of "Amazing Grace" began with a press of a button, I willed myself to hum along. I would find the words when they decided to come.

Keeping my eyes closed I felt the rhythm of the acoustic guitar accompaniment and visualized the words of what had to be the most beautiful song every written. The longer I recited the words in my head the further I was drawn into their meaning, their passion, and their reality.

"Twas grace that set me free..."

The religious intention of the words was not lost on me, but the song became my religion rather than the hallowed walls of any church or organized movement.

I felt the warmth of my tears racing down my face again but this time in awe rather than frustration. *Was this Fiona's God talking to me through lyrics?* If so, I wanted to know Him better. If not God, I wanted to be acquainted with the superior being these words represented.

This was greatness. This was passion. This was something my own father would believe in and that needed to be shared with the world.

Because the version of the song I selected held a twist the contemporary writer had included in the ancient hymn. A crescendo built, taking it with me.

"My chains are gone. I've been set free..."

The instrumentals rose and I felt myself rising with them. My eyes remained shut, but my arms lifted to the sky and I felt my body grow in the familiar power of music. This is where I belonged. It was a friendly place. A place all my own.

Finally the storm lessened into a calming peace, with it my body spent. I stood with head bowed in the middle of Room 3, drenched in my own sweat and tears.

Wow.

A distant applause, timid before building into an enthusiastic reward that all artists need to hear, brought me back to earth.

Oh, snap!

I forgot to lock the door and the class bell had invited the room's next occupant to enter. I looked to see a dozen or more students at the doorway, all clapping and yelling praise.

All this for a lone girl reacting to a song?

And then I realized what was really going on. I had not only reacted, I had participated.

It didn't take long for my fame to spread. Evidently my intended silent performance attracted the attention of every teacher, student, service worker, all the way down the staff roster. The big deal wasn't that I could sing…anyone familiar with my school knew singing was what I did. The point of the amazement was that not only did I sing, but that finally I was singing again.

Of course, now everyone expected me to speak and that just wasn't happening.…yet. Of course, few people gave me a chance to prove that one way or another because they were all talking for me, to me, and at me.

It came as no surprise when my mother met me at the front door after my walk home from school. Her eyes were bright with a fresh onslaught of tears and she trembled so visibly I feared for the safety of my baby brother who giggled at the unexpected motion of his mother's arms. I tossed my backpack toward the sofa and grabbed him up before Mom forgot to hold him close.

"Meri! Americka, is it true? Are you talking? Thank goodness!" As she spoke her hands were constantly caressing my arm, my face, my shoulder.

This was the most physical attention she had paid me since my return from the hospital. It seemed that touching made her hurt even more. I didn't realize just how much I had missed it until now. Cuddling my baby brother was comforting, but there was nothing like a mother's touch.

As grateful as I felt, I worried that her ministrations would end as soon as she understood I was not talking. But singing had to be a step in the right direction.

"I've already contacted the neurologist who treated you in the hospital and he said to bring you right in. So, go brush your teeth and we'll go."

It was obvious she had been waiting attentively for this announcement. Andy's diaper bag was packed and ready beside the front door, Mom's purse beside it with her car keys placed on top. As soon as I was ready, the Mom Taxi was prepared.

With one final hug, Mom breathed into my hair, whispering how much she loved me and how so very, very happy she was.

We rode to the hospital with the radio softly playing in the background and Mom excitedly chattering about who knows what. I occupied myself in the back seat with Andy, exchanging silly faces and inspecting the assortment of colored cereal bits spread out over the tray of his car seat. I do not think Mom realized I hadn't uttered a word to prove the truth of what she believed. Maybe it was just the idea of my unmuted voice and not the actual reality that was so upsetting to her.

Mom's consistent chatter appeared to be soothing to her without the input of others, so I just let her continue and hoped she would allow me to consult with my specialist without her in the room. Thinking this made me realize what a role reversal was happening between my mother and me.

Mothers exist to shield and protect their children, right? But now the child is concerned about protecting the mother from upsetting news. Because not hearing her daughter is complete and whole once again will surely be upsetting. I wish I could change the outcome of today's medical visit, but I knew in my heart what to expect.

Sure, I can sing, but I cannot yet speak. In the big scheme of the world that sounds like progress to me, but Mom is in need of instant gratification right now. Her life is upside down and the call from school seemed to point her in a more positive direction.

Maybe she will just keep talking and forget to test out my own vocal progress.

Listening to her go on and on, for a second I began to believe that may be a possibility. She just needed to live in her fantasy for a little longer.

Andy and I shared a conspirator's grin and began a new round of soundless patty cake.

11

IT IS WHAT IT IS

She wasn't too happy about it, but Mom allowed me to meet with the doctor by myself. Of course, my darling little brother held up his end of the bargain by demanding her immediate attention in both diaper and dinner demands. So, while she busied herself with that, I followed Dr. Rollins into an examining room and firmly closed the door behind me. My note pad at the ready, I narrated the turn of events in my situation as thoroughly as possible on the stenographer's paper.

She smiled and nodded as she read. Although she emitted one or two audible little hums, her perusal of the script was nearly as silent as if we were having a conversation in sign language.

"Okay, Americka. So you can sing, but you cannot talk. Well, that's something. But it's not unheard of. The trauma that caused all this is now allowing you to communicate in a way in which you are comfortable. You are a singer, so you sing."

I found it oddly comforting she wasn't overly concerned. Her almost nonchalant attitude matched my own and for that I was grateful. Mom wouldn't be as calm, of that I was certain.

"Do you think you could sing a little something for me?"

This was totally unexpected and since I had no idea how I had managed it before, I was very unsure of doing it again.

Seeing my confusion, Dr. Rollins smiled again and sat back in her chair.

"It's okay, Americka. If you did it once, it will happen again. I don't have any doubts of that. And you have ample witnesses from what I understand. Common sense tells me this happened because you were in your element. Calm, comfortable, and ready to exhibit something you do automatically. I think the best therapy for you is to spend as much time as possible in an environment similar to the music room at school." Dr. Rollins's words were encouraging, but I wasn't so certain Mom would see things this way.

As she was signing off on my chart, the music bubbled up and out of me in as close to perfect tune as I could muster. I kept my eyes tightly closed in order to control my pitch and regulate my breathing. The words just poured out, surprising both of us, but proving an important point. I could sing.

I opened my eyes and witnessed something that was probably a bit unusual for someone in the medical profession and not working with a life or death situation. Dr. Rollins was crying. Not in anguish or pain, but in a silent memorial stance.

"That was lovely, Americka. And your secret is safe with me. It will all work out. We'll just give it some time." She removed her glasses to wipe daintily at her eyes with a tissue before turning her attention back to me. "Post-Traumatic Stress Syndrome is nothing unusual and, in your case, will most likely take care of itself. We just need to be patient."

As my continued luck would have it, after she spent several minutes with the doctor while I entertained Andy, Mom's nonstop chatter continued all the way home, allowing me to remain silent for the ride and even into the evening.

Dr. Rollins's reaction to my revelation was odd, but then again, I was not the expert. She was.

So much for missing my voice, I thought. I mentally kicked myself for the sarcasm and was grateful for the further reprieve.

Since it was Friday, I knew the weekend promised to be challenging and I could only hope to hear from Fiona as a buffer. She hadn't answered my texts or e-mails telling her about my singing voice and I was beginning to get worried. Fiona wasn't prone to let me hang. But, I reminded myself, she was a college student with college student responsibilities. And she did have a part time job. She didn't really need a high school junior to baby sit.

But I still needed to talk to her and I definitely wanted to meet Daphne to pick her brain about the song that wouldn't leave my head. If the vocals on Fiona's CD were sung by her sister, there was obviously a relationship between song lyrics and singer and I would love to delve deeper into that.

Wow. It occurred to me I was actually entertaining the idea of singing in that silly talent show.

Mom decided she needed to take Andy for a walk and a trip to the baby store consignment shop sale after breakfast Saturday morning. Any verbal response from me was unnecessary after she overheard me rehearsing "Amazing Grace" in my room. With head phones on, I was deaf to my audience, but her wild clapping at the final note startled me into awareness.

"That was beautiful, Meri. It is so, so good to hear you singing again. I think you sound better now than you ever did!"

Mom rushed to put her arms around me and kissed me on top of the head just like Dad used to do.

"We're going to be okay, aren't we Americka?" Mom whispered into my hair before slowly stepping away from me, taking her time to keep her hands on me before wiping a stray tear from her own face.

When I assured her I didn't want to join her and I would be absolutely fine on my own (none of which I said, but only nodding my head in agreement when each question was posed), she waved from my bedroom door and proceeded to gather Andy and all of his required traveling gear. That kid certainly did not travel light.

I knew I had to get out of the house. This was my opportunity to find Fiona and share my news. After a quick check of my empty email inbox, I showered and dressed for my own outing.

I hadn't driven since the accident and was a little unsure of myself since the ink on my license was still practically wet. Never having been behind the wheel of the car alone, I momentarily second guessed myself. Just as quickly, I pictured Dad in the passenger seat and felt a bit stronger. Dad would be my co-pilot.

A bit more confident, my next step was taking his Jeep out of the garage. The Jeep had not been started since the explosion. I didn't even know if there was any gas in it. I also was uncertain as to her reaction if and when Mom discovered what I was going to do. I had to be back, safely tucked into my room, when she and Andy returned.

And leaving a note just would not suffice.

The Jeep keys were hanging on the peg beside the garage door, just like always. The police had returned Dad's vehicle from the destroyed movie theater days after the explosion. I hadn't realized until I entered the garage that a giant blue tarp now blanketed my father's prize Army-green two seater.

Easier to ignore that which we do not see.

After folding the tarp and placing it in a corner of the garage, I unlocked the Jeep door and climbed in behind the wheel. The unexpected fragrance of my Dad's cologne wafted up from the upholstery and I was hit with overwhelming grief. He was still here, in this car. I didn't want to think I would probably lose this last trace of him once the windows were down and fresh air provided a cleansing task.

I nearly stopped right then and re-covered the Jeep. Did I really want to sever this last physical connection with my dad?

While thinking this over, I realized starting the Jeep would not eliminate the smell and the Jeep really needed to be started anyway. It took several tries and I was cautious not to flood the engine in my attempts. I might be a rookie driver, but Dad had made certain I learned a few basic rules of car maintenance before hitting the road for the first time. I knew how to change a flat tire, check the oil, and all the little things involved in minor road side emergencies.

On the third try, the engine revved up and I sat back in the seat. The radio was tuned to an unfamiliar station and turned down low. But when I increased the volume I was so glad I was already in the sitting position. It was difficult for me to accept my hard rock Dad had been listening to this kind of music and since I had been the last passenger in his car, I knew he had not tuned in to this station.

As the beautifully harmonized words to "Amazing Grace" emanated in the dark confines of my father's Jeep, I had the creepy, yet comforting, feeling he was trying to tell me something. And that something was to go. To move forward. To steal his Jeep. And to find Fiona.

The Mall was located only a couple of miles from my house, but it felt like the drive took forever. I should have been arrested for driving under the speed limit. My caution took on a criminal intent. I was relieved to find a relatively empty parking lot and a parking place close to the main entrance.

The weather defined a day too lovely for inside activity, making my actions even more effortless. Luck was still on my side. Either it was too early for serious mall shoppers or the beautiful weather dictated other plans.

I just hoped Fiona was working today, or even better, that her twin was behind the counter at the book store. I was kind of excited to be challenged with the identical twin game. Would I know the difference? Who was sporting Goth today and whose day was it to present the pretty preppy attire of the obedient twin? In fact, the twins could have been scamming me all along.

The thought brought me up short until I realized how utterly ridiculous that sounded. They didn't have time to coordinate all the complicated detail that would entail. Did they?

When I approached the book store of their employ I did not see evidence of Goth or Prep, but there was a very handsome college age guy behind the counter. This had to be Daphne's latest hot crush.

This presented a big problem. With frozen vocal chords I had no way of asking about my friend or her sister. Writing a note was just too weird in this circumstance. I decided to wait it out and peruse the shelves for a while on the hope of one of the twins appearing.

I checked my watch, knowing my time was limited if I planned to sneak Dad's Jeep back in the garage without Mom the wiser.

Right at that moment I heard a familiar voice and looked in its direction eagerly.

"Good morning, Raymond," Fiona's mother had approached the handsome clerk and greeted him with familiarity.

"Mrs. White. Good morning. Good to see you." Raymond's voice was as alluring as his model-worthy appearance. "How is our girl?"

"She is doing better, Raymond, but I think she needs a few more days this time. Fiona's biggest concern is her job right now. I know her absence is not professional and that it puts you in a bind. She and I have talked it over and we both understand if you need to cut back on your hours." These last words were stated with an obvious hitch in her voice. What was going on? Where was Fiona? Why did she need more time off? And what was the meaning of Mrs. White's addition of "this time"?

The beautiful Raymond walked around the counter to put his arms around Mrs. White in an extremely "familiar" hug.

"Business is a little slow right now with spring break, so let her enjoy her own vacation from work." He held her as if this was not his first offering of comfort. "Is there anything I can do for *you* right now? You look like you could use a famous Raymond Fix and a good book. What say you? On the house." Raymond ushered Mrs. White in the direction of a cozy little cafe area that looked like the stage area for Mom's favorite old sitcom *Cheers.*

So far, she hadn't seen me and Raymond had barely acknowledged his sole customer. If my luck held out I could escape without a confrontation.

But at that moment, my luck came to an end. As I turned to make a hasty retreat, I miscalculated a turn in the stacks and ran full fledge into a display of bestsellers haphazardly arranged on a discount table. With paperbacks flying, I fell right into the mess I had made, making more noise.

With the accompaniment of concerned murmurs from Fiona's mother and the store clerk, I looked up in utter despair.

"Oh, my goodness! Americka? Is that you?"

Mrs. White reached a nicely manicured hand to her cheek before quickly extending it out to me. "Oh, dear, let me help you up."

Raymond shifted his gaze from me to the mess I had made and then to Mrs. White and back to me. I had probably ruined the better part of his morning, but he had mentioned a decline in patronage of late, hadn't he? All the more time to correct the damage I inflicted.

Mrs. White brushed off any imaginary lint from my fall and ushered me over to one of the over-stuffed sofas in the café area.

"Sit down here, sweetheart, and let Raymond get you a drink." And, oddly, Raymond went about doing just that. "I am so glad to see you, Americka. You might be exactly what the doctor ordered. Fiona would love to see you."

Raymond approached us with hands full of customized drink containers.

"Raymond, this is Fiona's friend, Americka. Isn't that a lovely name?" Fiona's mother handed me one of the signature beverages and smiled up at our server.

Raymond smiled back hesitantly and nodded in my direction.

"Americka was with Fiona during the explosion. They formed a nice little friendship. Americka has even attended church with us." Mrs. White tipped her cup in my direction in what I assumed was a silent salute.

"And Americka sings." She smiled at me over the rim of her cup and whispered to me or to herself, I wasn't sure, "Yes, she is just what we need right now."

12

ROLE REVERSAL

Mrs. White is so much like her daughter it isn't difficult to understand why Fiona is the awesome person that she is. When she understood my car dilemma she didn't pass judgment or chastise me. She simply paid our café bill and bid farewell to Raymond before instructing me to leave the Jeep at the Mall, She would return me after a little visit to Fiona.

I was guiltily just as excited to finally meet Daphne as I was to see Fiona. There seemed to be mystery surrounding my friend's "condition." I pondered on Mrs. White's choice of words of Fiona needing a few more days "this time." *What did that mean?*

Unlike my own mother, Fiona's mom let us ride without talk. The radio was tuned to what I would consider a contemporary church channel. The songs were soulful and full of uplifting praise. I made a mental note to research some of the band names later on my computer.

I must have been humming along because when Mrs. White turned into her driveway and shut the car motor, she spoke for the first time since we had left the mall.

"You have a lovely voice, Americka. I understand why Fiona is so adamant you share it with others." She covered the hand resting in my lap with one of her own and squeezed slightly. "Fiona is going to be so excited to see you. I promise I will get you home safe and sound."

The White's house was nothing like I expected, had I any expectations to make. My only encounter with Fiona's parents had been at church and they seemed a very humble couple. Fiona was a bit outrageous in dress and manner, but nothing prepared me for the underplayed extravagance of her home.

The exterior was a classic stone of the neighborhood, but the foyer gave away the obvious old money that was buried within. There was nothing abstract or pretentious about the gleaming wood work and the distinct smell of careful care that normally accompanies libraries and historic buildings. It was the smell of love and comfort.

Mrs. White led the way to the heart of the home: the kitchen. I did my best not to trip over my own feet as I gawked at the equally impressive rooms on either side of the hallway. There was nothing Kardashian about the home, but McMansion certainly hedged the description. There was some serious money here.

Fiona had never mentioned what her parents did for a living. From the looks of her and the level head she carried, there were no signs of a pampered or spoiled girl beneath that head. And she certainly did not live beyond the boundaries of goodness. Just the fact her family attended and participated in church and her sister sang gospel set the White family aside from the norm.

I followed Mrs. White into the largest, yet warmest, kitchen imaginable. The appliances were a gleaming brushed stainless steel and an array of polished pots and skillets hung from the exposed beams that floated above an enormous center floor island. The comforting aroma of spiced tea and cinnamon, fresh baked cookies, and yeasty bread met my nostrils. My mouth actually watered a bit and I found myself hoping my visit might include a taste of what I smelled.

So captured by the awesomeness of my surroundings, I didn't notice the small figure huddled at the corner of the massive kitchen island. She sat hunched over what appeared to be a steaming cup of something hot and probably the origin of that spicy perfume I first noticed upon entering the room.

"Fi, darling, you have company. Look who I found wondering around the mall!"

Mrs. White's voice had taken on a rather uncomfortable pitch and I thought she was going to cry.

When Fiona slowly lifted her head I felt the need to cry myself. Practically hidden beneath the confines of a knitted shawl she had successfully concealed her physical appearance, but in the light of day I could see the marks of something horribly wrong.

Her normally perfectly coiffed hair, whether in the prep or gothic mode, was ratted and obviously untouched by a brush. She had dark, dark circles beneath her cosmetic-less eyes and her cheeks were kind of sunken. Whatever was wrong with Fiona, she had aged in a strange, cinematic way. She looked horrible. She looked worse than sick. I hoped it wasn't contagious.

I don't think I could have created sound on a good day at that moment. I signed hello and plastered a weak smile across my face.

Fiona half-heartedly raised a frail hand in my direction and I glanced nervously at Mrs. White, whose concentration was solely on her daughter.

"I thought you would like to see Meri. You haven't been out of the house for days. Why don't you take your guest out to the garden and I will bring you a plate of cookies and some fresh tea." It wasn't a questioned request. Mrs. White was already busy preparing our snack as Fiona lifted herself with obvious effort from her perch.

Not knowing what else to do, I followed her to the far end of the kitchen and out the double French doors that lead to another breath taking area, this one outside and worthy of an artist's brush. When her mother mentioned sitting in the "garden" I did not expect the lushness of what I saw. This was no potato and lettuce patch. This was a full-fledged, White House-worthy rose garden. There were bird baths, a koi pond, and every imagined color surrounding the stone patio where we finally sank into the cushions of harem covered furniture.

Really? People really lived like this? This is what Fiona came home to every single day?

I was unsure what to do as I waited for Fiona's nonstop chatter to fill the empty space that would have echoed had it not been for the faint ripple of the little water fall that fed into the fish pond. She didn't even look at me, so signing was out of the question. I opened my mouth a dozen times but could not force a sound to come out.

We sat in silence for what seemed like hours, but was probably only a few minutes. Just when I began to think of creating a disturbance by throwing one of the clay flower parts, Fiona began to cry. A soft whimpering cry that grew into a wail.

I hurriedly rushed to her side and put my arms around her rigid body. Initially I felt physical resistance but just as quickly Fiona wrapped her arms around me and we rocked together in this mysterious bond of grief. She cried louder and harder and I held firm.

Before I could stop myself, I joined her tears. And, in that paradise of flowers and gentle fragrances, we cried.

13

WHAT TO DO, WHAT TO DO

I made it home safely an hour later, tucked in Dad's jeep for the night, and cleaned up any trace of the emotional visit I had at the White residence. I actually felt good, oddly cleansed. Fiona's sadness was a mystery to me, but somehow I knew it would all come to light with time.

Fiona's mom left us alone outside, but hurriedly rushed to the front door when she heard me make my departure. I got the feeling she had been watching from the confines of her beautiful home and was aware of all that transpired outside in her beautiful garden.

When she left me in the mall parking lot, she thanked me for coming and told me to come back again real soon. I left, with arms laden with warm ginger snaps I knew I couldn't explain to my own mother.

I had no idea what happened to cause Fiona's outburst. She hadn't said a word during all of our crying, but she had kissed me on the forehead before I left her alone in her grief. I felt like this was a typical Fiona action, even without knowing how true that was.

When I heard Mom return home, I quickly surrounded myself with school supplies in an attempt to appear studiously engulfed in academic concentration. As an added precaution I adjusted my head phones conveniently on my head to explain a lack of response to any questions she threw my way.

She still believed I could talk and I had so far successfully waylaid any explanation to the contrary. Mom was more content thinking the possibility of conversation on my part existed than the actual proof that it did. Weird.

I was really in a conundrum (thank you, honors English class) and had no idea how to behave around my own family. I had no idea what was plaguing Fiona. I couldn't talk to Janie or Holly (literally or figuratively). Lydia was not a possibility as she was nearly as high strung as my mother these days. Fiona was out of commission.

Dad was gone.

Andy talked better than I these days, but was incapable of sensible dialogue.

I was really, really alone to deal with something I didn't understand.

As I continued my pretend studies, I was aware of Mom looking into my room but saying nothing as she believed me to be absorbed in that mystical teenage land of loud rock music-infused study. Of course the headphones were silent so I could remain fully aware of my surroundings.

I needed a plan.

Suddenly it came to me. Tomorrow was Sunday. Fiona's church pastor was one of the neatest people I had ever met. If I could get to church in the morning without offering any explanation to Mom, maybe he could help me.

Hopefully, Mr. and Mrs. White would be there and even Fiona and I could finally meet Daphne. Their presence would make me feel a bit more welcome, although my past experience at the church had been nothing but welcoming. Fiona's church was a sanctuary of good feelings.

I had to smile at my own metaphor.

Sanctuary. That is what I needed right now.

When Mom knocked on my door two hours later to find me still pseudo immersed in my music and my studies she apologized for the interruption and set down a tray of dinner for me to eat at my leisure.

"I'm sorry you couldn't come down to join Andy and me for supper, sweetie. I didn't want to take you away from your homework. It looks like you're really busy." Mom peered over my shoulder to see what I was supposedly working on. "Oh, it looks complicated."

She patted my shoulder and then leaned in to place a light kiss on my head, near the spot where only hours before Fiona had done the same. It is said the human head is one of the most contaminated areas of the body and now mine contains the recent DNA of two of the most important people in my life. At least I'm covered in the event that I am needed in an episode of CSI.

"Andy is asleep and I am headed to bed myself. Don't stay up too late, Meri. I will see you in the morning."

And with that, any worries I had about being pressured to speak were dissolved. This was going to be easier than I thought.

According to the church bulletin I had kept from my last visit, there were three services. The first service began at 8:00 a.m. Mom would still be in bed when I left so a note to explain my whereabouts would not be unusual. The church was approximately a mile away, so I needed to allow time for the walk.

I could do this. I hurriedly tidied my "study" area and took a quick shower. All I had to do in the morning was leave a note to Mom, throw on some clean clothes, brush my teeth, and go.

I was becoming quite the renegade. Dad would be proud. I just hoped I would not dream about him tonight. I needed all of my wits about me to pull off what I had planned for the next morning.

Dad might have been proud of my initial planning, but, as any soldier knows, planning doesn't control the weather. It wasn't monsoon conditions, but the rain was falling quite steadily when I gently closed the front door at exactly 7:15 a.m. An umbrella would be helpful, but I knew I was destined to be a sloppy wet mess by the time I arrived at Sacred Sanctuary: The Church of Go. Maybe if I *had* dreamed about him, my dad could have helped me figure this out. But he had left me alone and comfortably dreamless.

Fortunately, there were few cars on the road at this time on a Sunday morning, so I didn't have to suffer additional road slop.

Other than the rain, the walk was enjoyable. I mentally put morning walk on my list of things to do in the future. It was rather therapeutic to be alone in the quiet of the day.

This early in the morning, the congregation was not as big as I remembered from the less traditional worship hour I had attended with Fiona. In fact, the 8 o'clock service was more of a reflection hour, what with the sparse number of attendees. But this was good for my cause because Pastor Hawkins would hopefully be less hurried and would have time for my unexpected visit.

And I was right. He even remembered me from my previous visit and was not at all taken aback with my notepad salutation.

"Hello, Americka! Welcome back. I am so glad to see you again."

His extremely casual attire was a bit confusing for the image of a man of God. This morning was even more extreme, probably a result of the weather. He obviously made no move to adjust his transportation and had ridden his Harley regardless of the wet driving conditions.

As he ushered me into his office, I could hear his leather riding boots squeak against the tile of the floor.

"How is your mother? The grieving process is a lengthy one and I know it seems your family will never be the same."

I sat in the offered leather chair and accepted the aromatic cup of steaming tea he handed me. Even his private space here was casual, but comforting.

"What can I do for you this morning?"

His question kind of took me off guard for a moment. *What could he do for me?* I had come for a reason, but for some reason it now eluded me.

Before I knew what I was doing, I scrawled a nearly illegible message on my note pad that I passed across the open space between our chairs and into his waiting hand.

"You want to sing?"

Wait. What?

"Fiona did mention that you are a singer. Our praise team would love to add a new voice to their ranks. I can arrange that."

If he found it odd that I could not talk, but that I wanted to sing, his smile did not waver and he didn't question my request.

"What else can I do for you, Americka? I don't think you hiked through the rain this early in the morning to ask permission to share your singing voice. Am I right?"

Still shocked at the turn of events my visit had taken, I nodded gravely and tried to control my writing hand so there were no more random requests spilling from my pencil lead.

The reverend did not laugh at my questions concerning my daydreams. In fact, he reassured me this was normal and not to read too much into the events that transpired in conjunction with those dreams. He did not once suggest my imagination was going haywire or that Dad was now a ghost nor did he sermonize or patronize my feelings. I actually felt like I had the first and best adult conversation of my life. Maybe even the only adult conversation. He made me want to stay, or at least come back sometime real soon. But duty called and he had to return to work and leave me to reflect on what we had talked about.

His main message was: Be patient. Be patient with Mom, with my voice, with my memories of Dad.

And, above all, don't stop singing.

I stayed for the last service, mainly to listen to the praise team, before gathering the impressive stack of reading material supplied by Pastor Hawkins: three musical scores to practice if I was serious about attending practice on Wednesday night, two pamphlets on death and dying to share with Mom, a schedule of small group sessions held at the church, a study schedule of scripture readings, and the *piece de la resistance*: A Bible of my very own. Not a hardcover sanctuary Bible. This was covered in a soft moleskin that had to be an expensive gift. I shook my head in refusal when he handed it to me, but he insisted and told me there was no price tag on the gift of salvation.

The rain had stopped and the sun shone for my walk home. Even with the weight of the materials I had collected, my steps felt lighter and the walk was over before I was ready to stop moving.

Of course the household was awake and on the move when I opened the front door. Andy was bouncing in his playpen while Mom tidied the already spotless kitchen. She was still sad, very sad, and no amount of cosmetics could conceal what I hoped were not permanent traces of tears on her face. But she was at least playing the game, trying to keep it together for Andy and me.

No wonder she wasn't aware of my lack of verbal participation. It was enough the doctor had checked me out and confirmed I was physically fine. She didn't really need proof. She had enough proof staring her in the face every day. When she looked at Andy, she saw a fatherless child. She looked at our house and saw a husbandless wife. Looking at me and seeing an emotionally scarred daughter was not in the equation. Denial at its best.

And as long as she needed this denial, the harder I would work to make it real for her.

I would keep my mouth shut.

Pastor Hawkins told me to be patient with my mother and with Fiona. I still had no idea what plagued my friend. The good reverend was tight lipped under some kind of pastoral-code of confidentiality, or maybe he didn't know...

Either way it didn't matter. He was doing his job in assisting the healing process for his congregation.

It felt good to be considered part of his fold.

After the obligatory head nods to my mother's announcement she was going to Lydia's for a while and would I mind staying with Andy while she got out, I arranged all of my new possessions around me on the floor beside my baby brother's playpen. It was nearly time for his afternoon nap, so this was to be an easy baby-sitting gig. I would read while he slept. There were worse ways to spend a Sunday afternoon.

I organized the pamphlets in one pile, the sheet music in another and finally placed the Bible study worksheets in another before gently placing my new Bible on the floor in front of me.

It was the most beautiful book I had ever seen. Not knowing much about church, but definitely capable of recognizing fine workmanship, I was aware of the monetary value of this book. Sacred Sanctuary was obviously a rather wealthy church to be able to gift such quality Bibles to just anybody.

It wasn't just the superb quality of the book that held me trans-fixed, though. The content of the Bible was more valuable than the beautiful moleskin cover. I just knew all the answers to any question I may have were within these pages and that reality made my fingers shake slightly as I gently opened my new book for a little light read-ing.

14

John Cougar, John Deere, John 3:16

Keith Urban's latest single blared from the radio in the kitchen the next morning when I entered to grab a quick breakfast before heading out to school.

I think the biggest adjustment in my mother's recent personality transformation had to be her love for everything totally in contradiction to her former preferences. Mom and Dad had always bowed reverently to classic rock music, so where this sudden penchant for all things country came from I wasn't sure. I didn't mind, though. There was no denying that country songwriters knew where to throw an emotional punch while offering sound philosophical advice.

I enjoy all music, so I didn't mind this turn of events. In fact the more I listened to country music, the more I liked it. This is NOT something I would share with Holly or Janie. They would not approve of the stigma associated with this musical preference.

Not that I shared much with my old friends. They had noticeably cooled their friendship jets of late. I guess the novelty of being associated with the girl who escaped the bomb was wearing off. They still followed me around at school like protective guard dogs, but with the final bell of the day their work shift was lifted and I didn't hear from them again until the next day. Thanks, friends.

Mentally slapping myself at this ungrateful sentiment, I tucked a granola bar in my back pack and bent at the high chair to kiss the only square of clean skin on Andy's head.

My little brother liked to share any meal with as much of his body as possible. But Mom insisted this was the only way he would learn to feed himself. And he seemed to enjoy doing it.

I noticed Mom sat a safe distance from him to avoid any offering he might want to share with her. But she looked content with her newspaper and fragrant cup of coffee. To avoid responding to her inquiry into my daily schedule, I stuffed an apple in my mouth after pausing to reproduce the kiss on the top of her head Andy had just received.

With a wave I entered an early spring morning that promised to spit on the Monday morning reputation of gloom.

I could not shake the Keith Urban song from my head and was so relieved to close the door on music practice room 3 at lunch hour.

I didn't know all the words to the song, but quickly found the lyrics on Google and listened to a loop of the song. By the fourth loop I had it down and opened my mouth to join in with some harmonies of my own.

This is when I realized that country music is really lyrical storytelling. The songwriter spoke of innocent youth, coming of age, and the realization that happiness comes down to the simple things in life. John Cougar represented the wild days of experimentation. John Deere farm equipment said something of the work value that Americans developed.

And John 3:16 is probably one of the world's best known Bible verses: For God so loved the world that he gave his one and only Son, that whoever believes in him shall not perish but have eternal life.

This philosophy put my own to shame. I couldn't wait to get home and read for myself that particular chapter in my new beautiful Bible.

The very title of this song was like an outline for living a happy life.

Weird.

When the bell dismissed me from my hour of contemplation, I left the music room with a lighter heart, but a full head.

"OMG, Meri, what are you doing? Are you singing?!"

Holly's screeching question caught me totally off guard as we walked to our next class.

"Ewwww…and is that a country song?"

Yes, dear Holly, I thought. I haven't spoken a word in weeks and the first words out of my mouth in your presence are totally not socially acceptable.

I didn't even bother to register the distaste on her face, but walked directly into fifth period math to learn more about algorithms as if what had just happened was anything but unusual.

15

PIZZA AND PRAISE TEAM PRACTICE

I had actually forgotten about praise team rehearsal until Wednesday after school. It was becoming increasingly more difficult to avoid talking to Mom, so any excuse to escape from her presence was welcome. She seemed to be doing a bit better mood-wise and I didn't want to upset the proverbial apple cart with my noncompliance in communication.

So, I left a note before supper time telling her I would grab a bite to eat at church after rehearsal. Pastor Hawkins had told me that Wednesday night was pizza night in the church's hospitality room. I tucked a couple of dollars in my back pocket to contribute to the offering and grabbed my old bicycle out of the garage.

Holly would just love this. We used to ride bikes together a lot when we were in elementary school, but this mode of transportation just wasn't cool now in our later years. I didn't really care if it was cool. I just wanted to cut my travel time in half.

And I actually liked my bike. Dad and I had picked it out during a visit home before his last deployment to the Middle East. I remember telling him it looked fast enough for me to peddle it all the way to him if I had to.

Granted the bike was pretty fancy, but I understood better now why my comment had brought him to tears through his laughter.

Because Dad named everything he owned, he had named my bike Henrietta. Why, I do not know, but I had insisted the name was too long and we settled on Henri with a French accent.

So when Henri and I pulled in front of Scared Sanctuary, my first quandary was where to secure my very special bike.

"Just wheel her inside!" A voice from above shouted out at me in answer to my silent question.

Before I could totally freak out at this supernatural occurrence, I looked up in the direction from which the voice came and saw Pastor Hawkins waving from a second floor window.

"Hello, Meri! Glad you could come. Just put your bike inside the front doors and head into the sanctuary for a short prayer time before the fun begins."

There was no doubt I was a little shaken by what I thought was a voice of divine providence and not a mere mortal representation of that deity.

"Get it together, Americka. You're freaking me out."

I didn't realize I had spoken the words out loud until another voice, this time right behind me, offered a reply.

"Yep, and talking to your self isn't freaky? Just so you don't answer yourself, I guess."

The voice was slightly familiar, but when I turned in its direction I was not prepared to see Raymond.

"Looks like Pastor Larry is true to his word, not that I doubted him. He said he would do some recruiting for us."

All I could do was stare at him. First of all, this was Raymond from the book store. Secondly, and should have been firstly, I just spoke. In **front** of a person. He didn't seem to find this unusual, but inside I was jumping up and down with excitement. *I could speak!*

"Hey, Ray-Ray, get yourself in here. We are in need of some technical assistance!" A chirpy voice met us at the vestibule, causing Raymond to wave absent-mindedly in that direction, but never taking his eyes off of me. And his eyes were disturbingly of that romance novel melting-into variety.

"Welcome, Americka. I'll see you in the sanctuary." And with that he left me leaning against my trusty bike, still stunned at the fact that words had left my mouth.

Following Pastor Hawkins' promised brief prayer time, the fun really did begin. I was truly convinced that Sacred Sanctuary was a place of miracles and talented people. No wonder it was nicknamed the Church of Go. Everyone seemed to want to *go* there. There didn't seem to be any trace of jealousy or competition. It seemed like everyone was more anxious to share the other's talents and gifts than to show case their own.

When I thought of Pastor's explanation of Sacred Sanctuary's nickname, I chuckled to myself. He had told me about a roadside sign he had seen while studying to be a minister. His travels had taken him to a ramshackle town where part of his seminary assignment was to help organize a youth group at the Church of Go. The "d" had fallen off the church marque. Rather than fixing that mistake, Pastor Larry had taken this opportunity to include this message in the youth group curriculum.

Allowing this to roll around in my brain, I listened to and even joined the ranks of the harmony section of the praise team. It was awesome. Jeremey, the youth director, handed me a CD of the most sung songs to listen to on my own time. The Church of Go. I could certainly understand the attraction of that sentiment.

I couldn't remember having this much fun before. I really felt like I had found my second home.

Walking toward the wall where I had parked my bike, I almost missed it. The ornate portrait frame was actually one of the only formal accessories to this otherwise rather modern building. It reminded me of "old" money. The image it framed, though, made me breathless.

It was Fiona. Posed elegantly and looking right at me.

I wanted to ask one of the departing participants about the portrait, but there were no words left in me. As un-expectantly as I had spoken to Raymond earlier, I was suddenly mute once again.

Beneath Fiona's face was a proof that took my own breath completely away.

Inscribed in delicate font I saw:
Daphne Renee White
Taken too soon.
May 1, 1997-2014.
May her song forever be heard.

16

May 1, 2014. Exactly one year to the day of meeting Fiona in that dingy theatre restroom on the most fateful day of my life.

I had been suffering through a war movie with my dad. How I wished I could suffer through another one.

She had been supposedly tolerating her own painful cinema afternoon by sharing a chick flick with her twin sister, who ironically was not even there. She was dead. *And had been for a year.*

And now Fiona was reliving her sister's death in some kind of morbid anniversary. Is this what I could expect in another few months when the day my dad died is relived in what will undoubtedly be a media celebration of sorts?

Did this mean that Fiona was suffering some kind of psychotic condition? Was she dangerous? To herself? To other people?

Wow.

Who was Fiona?

With this very disturbing news, I was prompted to finish the project of moving Ralph to his new residence in my room. Mom did not seem to notice the vacant space in the kitchen from where I had removed Dad's computer. If she did, she evidently wasn't bothered by it.

With Ralph fully in place on my desk, I was now ready for high power wireless internet and I had the world at my fingertips. I refused to clean the surface of Ralph's keyboard so that my fingertips were touching the last remaining surface that my dad had touched.

Reason told me this idea was silly, but every time I typed on his keyboard, I felt like Dad was holding my hand.

Upon Googling the White family I was not surprised by the overwhelming response. White was an extremely common name, but this was not an extremely common family. The proof grew before me in graphic, cybernetic color.

Randal White, Fiona's father, was heir to one of the largest coal mining family fortunes on the East coast. Not a coal miner himself, his investment prowess lead to an even cushier fortune. That explained the lavish lifestyle of the White estate. Because after visiting there, there was no better description for Fiona's house. It was undoubtedly an *estate*.

Evidently Mrs. White contributed her own finances to the wealth of the family. Winona Blanch White was not an heiress, but a millionaire in her own rite. After graduating from a small all-girl college, Winona found her fortune by recording praise sound tracks that were used all over the world as part of the initial praise team movement in contemporary church services.

So that explained the music niche shared by Fiona and her sister. It also quantified the family's devotion to their church. With the yearly monetary gift the White family donated Sacred Sanctuary, The Church of Go was able to employ top notch sound equipment and fund extended youth programs across the state. No wonder Daphne's portrait was so publicly displayed. Not only was she an instrumental member of the church music program, her family also pretty much owned the church.

And now she was dead.

If I wasn't speechless before, I certainly was now.

But I had some silent digging to do. Fiona was surrounded by so many mysterious questions, but I seemed to have discovered the core of her mystery.

Birchwood Gazette *Sunday, May 3, 2014*
The daughter of prominent Birchwood citizens
Randal and Winona White has died. Early Satur-
day morning, young Daphne Renee White was

found unresponsive at the home of friends following a sleepover event. Details are unknown as to cause of death at this time. The family has requested an autopsy. Ross Funeral Home is in charge of entombment arrangements and details will be disclosed at a later time. Condolences should be directed to daphnerenee.ross.

Ralph should have been steaming with all the exertion I put him through. Thank goodness Mom assumed that all of my computer work was due to a school research project. A die-hard stickler for academic responsibility she didn't dare interrupt my investigative work, creating a no-talk environment and saving me further exertion on my acting abilities.

I was glad to have my dad beneath my fingertips as I dug deeper into Fiona's family tragedy.

Although Fiona did not appear to be the uppity, spoiled child of excessive wealth, it seemed her identical twin sought attention in a different walk of life. Daphne was the party girl. Of that I was certain after unearthing multiple reports of her presence in less than acceptable situations that involved outrageous parties and even police involvement.

Only once did I find a report of the White twins together in a reported situation. Fiona wasn't mentioned again in connection with her sister's shenanigans.

I had to wonder if Fiona's explanation of the Goth vs. preppy dress code was her way of representing the extreme differences in her and her twin. Or was this something the girls had actually done in order to protect them against public scrutiny?

Whatever the reason, Fiona's explanation made sense and was very believable. Was this her way of protecting Daphne? Or was this the result of the deep seeded denial she suffered at the loss of her twin?

By the time Dad and I had typed our way through everything White family- related, I was emotionally exhausted.

Poor Fiona. All this time I had believed her to be such a happy, quirky college girl, looking for a possible protégé. But, no, Fiona was in search of a replacement for her birth right.

This put me in a quandary. I had no idea how to approach my friend with the knowledge I had accumulated without her assistance. She probably attached herself to me because I knew nothing about her past and it was easy to continue to pretend that Daphne was alive in the reality of my ignorance.

As I prepared for bed, I thought about my options. I had no idea where to go with my newfound knowledge.

It came to me quite unexpectedly, after letting it marinade in my mind for nearly an hour.

I had to talk to Raymond.

He would certainly have some answers. And I wouldn't mind the opportunity to gaze into those lovely eyes again.

17

Dulcimers, A Gorgeous Guy, and Amazing Grace

After securing my bike at the Mall bike rack outside a side entrance, I discovered that The Book Barn was surprisingly busy on Friday evenings. Mom had no problem with me biking to the mall for what she assumed was a gal's night out with Holly and Janie. So far I had not lied to her, but I still felt guilty about her blind trust in me. She had no idea that Holly and Janie had pretty much dumped me long ago. Or maybe it was the reverse, I realized suddenly. My school hood friendships felt rather shallow in the wake of my life now.

After a little more snooping on the internet, Ralph led me to some more interesting information about the White family. The Book Barn was actually owned by the family and was Mrs. White's attempt at holding a job outside of the house. She worked the hours not reserved for her daughters. Raymond Welch was the only other paid employee.

I felt like there must be some kind of family relationship there between Raymond and his source of income, but that detail didn't hold any urgency for me right now. I needed to find out more about how I could help Fiona. I felt like Raymond held some answers and I sincerely hoped that his work hours included Friday evenings.

Luck was on my side. Again.

At first I didn't see Raymond in the center of a rather impressive pack of flirtatious females. And that was exactly what it was. A Flirtatious PACK of females. From lollipop licking tykes to giggling preteens, vying with a couple of high school cheerleader types and even a delicately made-up older woman, Raymond was surrounded by his evening customers. I wondered what Mrs. White would make of her employee running her business from a pedestal of admiration.

Just as I told myself that maybe this was not a very good time to vie for Raymond's attention, I heard my name and realized I had been seen. Raymond beckoned me to join him in the huddle that formed around him.

Not knowing exactly what to expect, I was definitely surprised to see an odd looking musical instrument placed across his knees where he sat perched on a tall metal stool. His right hand strummed the four strings that stretched the length of the beautiful wooden instrument body while he gently placed his fingers strategically on a variety of frets to form musical chords.

He continued strumming and chording as his eyes met mine and he began to sing.

"Amazing Grace, how sweet the sound; that saved a wretch like me."

Raymond winked at me and nodded in a silent request.

I didn't even give it a second thought, but opened my mouth and sang the second line of what had become my new favorite song.

He joined me on the third line and we harmonized until the end of the first verse.

He didn't even have to encourage me to sing the second verse solo, with him joining in with his own harmony on the chorus. And then he did something wonderfully unexpected. Raymond sang words that didn't belong in the original hymn but that concluded the sentiment in a beautifully contemporary fashion.

As if we had rehearsed this song hundreds of times before, Raymond and I sang one final verse of "Amazing Grace" to end our impromptu performance.

I wasn't even certain I was breathing at the sound of the last chord and when my eyes met his, I knew Raymond was experiencing the same exhilaration. In keeping with his working responsibility, he recovered first and addressed his customers.

"And that's how it's done, ladies. I cannot guarantee the quality of singing that comes with this dulcimer will be of the same caliber, but I have no doubt that you will produce beautiful music with this fine instrument. I am very excited that Mrs. White agreed to include this element of local culture to our already fabulous Book Barn. So, if any of you wish to experiment with the cardboard replicas in the sitting area, please do so. A schedule of dulcimer lessons is listed on the monthly newsletter found on the coffee table. Be sure to take one with you."

With that, his admirers dispersed to touch the practice instruments arranged on the floor around the sofa and overstuffed arm chairs in the café portion of the store. I breathed, finally, a sigh of relief. Whether it was in response to no longer being the center of attention or because I had Raymond to myself. I wasn't sure.

"Well, hello there, Miss Meri. You saved the day for sure and certain," Raymond tipped an imaginary hat brim in my direction before hopping off his stool and carefully sitting the dulcimer on a nearby countertop.

I wanted to ask about the dulcimer, but suddenly found myself mute once again. Instead I traced my fingers across the smooth wood finish on the instrument's casing. Carved near the neck were two delicate hummingbirds and again at the base of the fret board were two small hearts.

Although I had never seen one in person, I was familiar with this Appalachian stringed instrument and excitedly wondered if I could learn to play it. I reminded myself to snatch up one of those lesson schedules before leaving the book store. I didn't imagine that I could afford a dulcimer of my own, as I knew most were hand made by Appalachian artisans who chose the finest woods in crafting their instruments. But I thought I could handle playing a cardboard replica for a while. Common sense told me that fools rush into impulse buying before thinking through the results of their decisions.

I remembered the insanely ridiculous coat Holly had insisted her mother purchase for her winter coat when we were in the sixth grade. The maxi coat was beautiful, yes, but not at all practical. Made of a brushed suede material, it did have a hood, but only a thin faux silk lining.

Holly nearly froze to death that winter. But not once did she utter a word of regret for forfeiting a suitable winter coat in the name of fashion. While the rest of our class enjoyed a season of sled riding parties and snow ball fights, Holly pretended to prefer sitting home polishing her nails. It was a long winter for Holly, but the following year she proudly displayed her winter white parka with a fur lined hood and puffy insulation.

Too bad we had no snow that winter. The lesson of Holly's winter coat was deeply imprinted on my brain. Thank you, Holly.

"So, what do you think? Should we start recording together?" Raymond's question interrupted my reverie and it was actually only when I felt his fingers rest lightly on my hand did I realize that my mind had wondered to a different time and place.

"You think we're ready for the big time?" Hearing my own voice startled me even more.

"So, Miss Meri has words without notes. I was beginning to wonder if it was just me, or you didn't talk to anyone but Fiona."

At the mention of her name I detected a slight break in Raymond's voice that reminded me of my purpose.

"Have you seen her?" I asked before Raymond shut down.

He nodded his shaggy head and busied himself tidying around the cash register. I guess if I wanted any more information I had to push some more words out of my mouth.

"So, Raymond, do you know what's going on with her? What happened to her sister? Did you now Daphne? What was she like?"

Raymond shook his head this time and harshly wiped at the dustless glass of a showcase.

"Too many questions, little girl. Too much sadness for an otherwise lovely day. How 'bout a latte? I make a mean fat-free iced caramel that puts Starbucks to shame."

And that appeared to be all that I was going to get from Raymond for the time being. I had nothing else to do so I could play his game until he kicked me out the store, but I really didn't want to get on his bad side.

I liked Raymond. He was funny and smart and talented and, yes, drop-dead gorgeous. Plus he knew about my friend and he was probably the only avenue of information I was likely to travel. And, amazingly, I could talk in front of him. I know my mother would accuse me of crushing and the doctors would associate this with some sort of emotional trauma and rush me into counselling.

I decided I was just comfortable. Raymond did not represent a need to please.

The rest of the morning and early afternoon I spent browsing the shelves and actually getting emotionally lost in the collection of rare and used volumes, many of which were kept behind glass walls for protection. Mrs. White really liked books. The addition of this beautiful display of collector's items made that clear.

I found a massive assortment of religious material tucked away in a quiet corner near the rear of the store. I was just marveling over the colorful display of moleskin Bibles when the sound of tinkling bells announced the arrival of yet another customer. Raymond was very busy today.

My hand hovered over a brightly bound purple Bible when a familiar voice practically screeched my name.

"Meri! You're here!"

Fiona's arms wrapped tightly around me before I had a chance, mentally or physically, to register her presence.

"I'm so glad I found you. Your mother said you went to the mall with friends, but I found that hard to believe after the way they treated you last time. You have discovered the best kept secret in town, though. Between Ray-Ray's entertaining barista moves and my mother's love for family, this is the place to be."

Fiona didn't release me from her crushing hug but bent her mouth closer to my ear to whisper loudly, "We even have a knitting circle that meets here. Something for everyone, that's what you'll find at the Book Barn."

Fiona released her arms from around me but kept a hand firmly attached to my shoulder.

"Isn't that right, Ray-Ray? Whip me up one of those caramel things while I show Americka where we stash the Saturday pastries."

I glanced in Raymond's direction and realized his face mirrored my reaction to Fiona's arrival.

I was so relieved to see her and to hear her comforting rambling, but there was something almost manic with her behavior.

By the time Fiona's coffee was ready and the two of us were armed with a plate of the fancy pastries reserved for the Saturday morning crowd, the store had cleared out for the first time in over an hour. With the plate of goodies placed in the middle of the large coffee table in the sitting area, we slumped into the overstuffed chairs and put our feet up.

"So, what have you been up to? I am so sorry that I was too sick to visit the other day. Don't know what it was, but I'm all better now. And we need to get ready for the big show. Have you been singing?" Fiona gingerly dabbed at her blood red lips to remove any pastry crumbs without smearing the cosmetic stain.

"Has she been singing?!" Raymond questioned as he joined us with his artfully prepared caramel concoction. "This girl is a gold mine, Fi! I haven't heard a voice like hers since..." Raymond's excitement faltered and he looked down at the cookie he had just scarfed off the table.

"Well, I haven't heard anything that lovely in a long while." I noticed Raymond glanced rather worriedly in Fiona's direction.

Whatever he was worried about was unheeded, though. Fiona continued rambling in response to his initial words.

"You're singing! Meri, that's great. I can't wait to hear."

Not missing a beat, Fiona jumped from her cushioned seat to retrieve a guitar on a stand behind a potted fichus tree.

"Let's sing!"

And that's what we did until Raymond signaled it was closing time.

We sang.

18

HEALING

Mom and Andy were not home when I return ed to the house after a very unusual and unexpectedly enjoyable afternoon with Fiona and "Ray-Ray." Even with the cutesy nickname I was beyond certain Mom's theory of me "crushing" would be entirely accurate. Raymond was the sweetest, most sincere boy I had ever met. Besides my dad, of course.

I still had no idea what his connection with the White family was, but there was clearly a strong tie in existence.

I was disappointed I hadn't had time alone with him for further interrogation into Fiona's situation, but the time we spent together was enough to fill the void for now.

While waiting for Ralph to boot up, I prepared myself a little snack to keep me sustained while waiting for Mom to return from her errands.

Since I had already been investigating the White family, there were search tabs already set on the computer and all I had to do was encourage a further search into the family's history. Daphne's death seemed to be an ongoing mystery, at least to me, and something that obviously held the key to Fiona's state of mind.

The first article I brought up threw me for a full loop.

A grainy newsprint photograph of Daphne and Raymond stared at me from Ralph's oversized screen. An arm draped over Daphne's shoulders, Raymond smiled at the photographer in what appeared to be overwhelming happiness. Daphne posed prettily for the picture, but didn't seem to share the devotion I saw in Raymond's eyes.

The realization there was a romance between the two crept into my brain and I was suddenly filled with guilt. Only moments before I had been entertaining the idea of that very relationship for myself.

Were Daphne and Raymond a couple before she died? Was he the boy Fiona referred to on the day of the bombing?

But that wouldn't make sense. Daphne was already dead when Fiona and I met. She wasn't attending the scornful chick flick with her twin on that day. Fiona had been watching the movie alone.

Instead of attempting to unravel this new mystery, I hurriedly Googled Raymond Welch. His bio was typical of a teenage guy except for the fact that Raymond's family seemed to be equally as wealthy as the Whites. Son of a retired NASA engineer, Raymond was the only child of Harold and Martha Welch. Until his sophomore year in high school, Raymond had attended a private school in New England. When his mother was diagnosed with breast cancer the family moved here to be closer to Martha's lifelong friend, Winona White.

Okay, so *there* was the connection I had been looking for. Raymond's mother and Fiona's mother were childhood friends and Martha wanted to be near her friend during her trials with cancer. It was a comfort thing. And it seemed to work both ways. While Winona was there for Martha, Martha became a comfort in Winona's time of need.

I wondered if Mrs. White felt beholden to her friend enough to give Martha's son a job.

I flipped back to the picture of Raymond and Daphne on the previous internet page. Was their romance also in obligation to this friendship?

"Get a grip, Meri. Your imagination has taken on a totally cynical side."

I didn't realize my inner thought had muttered its way into the atmosphere until I heard footsteps stopping at my door.

"Did you say something, Americka?"

My mother swayed slightly under the growing weight of baby Andy, who was draped in slumber across her shoulder.

Andy had obviously had an active day on their outing and Mom was not anxious to wake him right now. She waved slightly in my direction before tiptoeing towards my little brother's room to tuck him away for the night.

I was beginning to believe I could ride this mute condition for a long, long while at this rate. I was also beginning to realize maybe this was part of Mom's denial phase of dealing with Dad's death. So, maybe it wasn't such a bad thing after all. It was just part of her healing process.

I wasn't offended. Just concerned.

Evidently she had just heard my voice, so that meant I really could talk. I guess I was healing as well.

That night I dreamed about my father. The last time I saw him I had been escaping his war movie, without giving his feelings a thought. I just wanted out of that cinema and away from the loudness of war. The last time he had visited me in dream land, we had been in his college dorm room. Physically quiet, but emotionally charged with some unseen battle.

In this dream I stood by his side in an active war zone. The noise was deafening, even more so than the Hollywood effects on the movie screen.

He couldn't hear me as I tugged at his military flak jacket, trying to pull him away from the ugliness that unfolded in front of us. In my dream I begged him to look away, to forget about his duties as a service man and to come home to his family. If he heard me, he made no indication. He didn't even notice me.

The crashing of artillery fire deafened me but did not appear to faze my father. He peered fearlessly at the field of mortal destruction that lay before us. I had to wipe desperately and constantly at the tears pouring from my swollen eyes and tried to make him look away. But he persisted as I witnessed the blood bath that unfolded on the field of battle.

I didn't know what to do.

Not once, not twice, but three times did he visit these unholy lands to watch his comrades fall at the sacrifice to their flag and to America's philosophy of fighting for freedom and honor.

These measures could, and would, supposedly protect America from further massacre in the form of such crisis we witnessed on the day of September 11, 2001. Why America has to get involved in such madness was inexplicable.

I screamed my own protests and begged my dad to wake up and go back home with me where his family and friends need him. All of this in the sake of freedom. Whose? Ours? His? The suicide bombers with no concern for human life?

I didn't understand. I would never understand.

Before waking in the clammy sweat that accompanies fear, the last thing I saw was my father saluting the flag and smiling toward the horizon. This was his destiny. This was his purpose as a United States soldier.

Most of the time I do not remember my dreams and I don't really know if I dream much at all.

But the image of my dad standing at attention in the foreground of such a grisly scene brought me to an abrupt waking. I did not need to give this dream too much scrutiny. I knew exactly what he was trying to tell me.

I needed to heal.

So, I saluted my alarm clock and prepared to do just that.

19

THE UNSPEAKABLE

"I was with her the night she...that night."

Raymond's voice was loud and clear and I tingled at the possibility of hearing the full, unedited truth about Daphne Renee White.

"Yes, she and I had a special friendship. I think I wanted it to be more serious than she did, but it didn't really matter. I love, loved, Daph. Her family is like a second family to me. Daphne and Fiona are my best friends. It's like they are an extension of me."

Raymond's voice cracked a little and I heard him ask for some water.

Instead of singing in practice room 3 today, I listened to a recorded police interview I had found on the internet.

I felt weird listening to it at home. For some reason, my private musical oasis felt like a better fit for undercover endeavors. This is where I uttered my first song voice. This is where I vented when home wasn't an option. The walls of this private room heard more of my anguish over losing a parent, losing a best friend, and losing the ability to communicate than any human ear.

Connected to the high-power school-issue headphones, I spread my lunch around me and hunkered down on the sound-absorbent carpeted floor to listen to what Raymond had to say about the night Daphne White died.

"Her sister, Fiona, didn't want to go to the party and I really wasn't all that interested myself. But Mrs. White didn't like for her daughters to go to social functions unescorted. And I had a bad feeling about the party host. I knew him from around the halls at school, but he wasn't someone I would normally buddy with. He was more into sports and didn't seem to be receptive to an afternoon talking about the classics or jamming in my basement."

There was a pause and I could hear the turning of notebook paper and the swooshed sound of someone adjusting themselves on an upholstered surface.

"What do you mean when you say, er, 'jamming'?" An unfamiliar voice interjected to fill the void of silence on the recording.

Even though the interview was on-line, there was no visual. So I had to rely on my imagination to fill the gaps when silence ensued.

"Oh, sorry."

"That's okay. I just need clarification."

"Sure." Raymond cleared his throat and probably took another sip of the provided water before continuing. He might have been silently biting his tongue at the musical ignorance of the interviewer, but he was ever the polite young man.

"Jamming is the term musicians use when a group of them just hang out and play. Their respective instruments, I mean. Play their instruments. There is usually nothing organized about the event and it gives everyone a chance to contribute. It's just fun."

Another brief gap of silence as the interviewer absorbs Raymond's response.

"So, on the night in question, you agreed to escort Daphne White to the social event hosted by a fellow classmate. But you really weren't excited about attending yourself. Is that correct?"

Suddenly I felt like I had mistakenly uncovered a trial segment and not a newspaper interview. It sounded so formal and rather intimidating. Maybe Ms. Kenzie Jones, the interviewer, was feeling the heat to improve her interview techniques.

"Yes, that is correct. I did not want to go to the party. But I didn't want Daphne going alone."

"So, being the devoted boyfriend that you are, you joined Daphne in order to save your reputation as a couple."

"Whoa, Ms. Jones, this had nothing to do with my relationship with Daphne. It was just a party."

I guess Raymond was feeling the interrogation portion of this interview was misplaced, just like I did. Ms. Jones needed to save this mode of questioning for the court room.

"I am so sorry, Raymond. I just want to make sure this interview accurately represents what happened on the night of Daphne White's demise. Let's continue, if that's okay with you."

You go, Ray-Ray. Turn the tables on uppity Ms. Jones.

I had to laugh at myself in this cheerleader role. No one else could even hear what I was hearing and there was no one near with whom to debate this interview.

But I was getting closer to finding out the truth since no one else involved in this great mystery was willing to talk.

After Fiona appeared at the Book Barn yesterday, there was not another opportunity to question Raymond and from his reaction when I first mentioned Daphne, there wasn't much of a good chance he was willing to open up further anyway.

This was my only means of discovering what was going on. And I needed to know in order to reach out to Fiona, as she had reached out to me. No matter what, this strange girl had etched a solid place on my heart and my mind. She was a true friend.

Just as the taped interview resumed, I felt the vibration of the class bell. With the headphones on it was difficult to hear, but the sudden rustle of movement outside the soundproof walls supported the evidence of time to go. I reluctantly shut down the equipment I used and carefully placed the headphones back in the appropriate cubby before cleaning up my impromptu picnic on the floor and leaving my sanctuary until tomorrow.

I knew I really needed to use this time for rehearsal, but using the impressive school sound equipment was just too tempting to pass up.

Yesterday I had totally committed myself to Fiona's wish to enter the contest. In fact, the three of us were going to work on it as a trio of sorts. Raymond would definitely provide the instrumentals and

Fiona was still thinking about her part in the performance. For right now, she was acting manager/agent. She would handle the paperwork end of the venue and schedule our rehearsal time. It was laughable how excited she was about the entire event, but there were butterflies in my stomach at the thought of working so closely with Raymond. I knew I had to work on my feelings where he was concerned.

Raymond belonged to Daphne, or at least to her memory. It would not do to become involved in some morbid romantic triangle, especially when a key player in the drama was dead.

It took me most of the week, but I finally got the whole disturbing story, via internet; so the accuracy may be a little sketchy. But it was enough for me to fill some pieces and understand more thoroughly what I was dealing with. Nothing could change the fact that Fiona's twin sister was dead, leaving her wallowing in guilt she had not been there to alter the events that unfolded that night. Nor could it ever erase the image Raymond fostered in his own mind.

According to my on-line sources, when Fiona White refused to join her sister and their mutual friend Raymond Welch, the two partygoers supposedly left the White residence at 8:00 p.m. on the night of May 1, 2014. Witnesses confirmed the couple's ETA and had no reason for concern.

In the wealthy neighborhood where the party was set, it was not unusual for a resident to host a teen party. Parents adhered to the belief they would rather have their children home in the event of disorderly conduct or illegal drinking and driving. They seemed to feel this was a logical compromise to the inevitable actions associated with coming of age events.

In most cases, the parents or guardians of the hosting teen were present somewhere on the property during the time of the festivities. Whether it would have made a difference or not, I don't know, but on this particular night the parents of the football star hosting the party had gone to a function elsewhere. They had trusted their son to behave.

Unfortunately, trustworthy was not a quality identified with the graduating senior in charge. He was anxious to leave high school and more than anxious to move on with his college football scholarship that would take him hundreds of miles from family. This was another reason for the massive celebration that drew Daphne to his home. In three weeks they would be graduates embarking on another chapter of their life. One that she, too, was excited to experience.

I know, deep in my heart, Fiona wanted to believe Daphne's death was an accident. Something not planned, not pre-meditated. But all indications showed that on this fateful night, Daphne Renee Smith willingly participated in extensive consumption of alcohol and experimental drug use.

Bowing to the pressure of fitting in with the celebratory atmosphere, Raymond succumbed to imbibing as a drinking participant and at some point was separated from his companion. By the time he rejoined Daphne, she was active in a rambunctious drinking game with other members of the football team. At this time Raymond realized things were getting out of hand and he encouraged Daphne to leave with him. She refused and continued partying.

The next thing Raymond remembered was standing over an unconscious Daphne, begging her to wake up.

He insisted medical help be called, much to the severe opposition of the majority of the partiers. When he called 911 things got ugly and he was forcefully removed from the house. He met the paramedics and local policemen at the front gate of the estate and was instantly placed in the back seat of the cruiser where he remained until he and more than half of the attendees were hauled off to be incarcerated until parents and guardians could retrieve their wayward children.

It was evidently a big joke to most of the students and many of the parents who viewed this as just another rite of passage for their graduating seniors.

Little was made of the event. Even when Daphne did not regain consciousness and remained unresponsive in the hospital emergency room. Her death was a media event. The prestigious residents of town managed to underplay it, though, in an attempt to keep negative publicity from their families and the town itself.

This was viewed as a sad disclosure of poor decision making and chalked up as a hard lesson in the scheme of life.

Hundreds attended Daphne's funeral and the sincerity of remorse eased the souls of the media frenzy. But for Raymond and the White family, there was nothing that could soothe the loss of a young girl's life. And it left both Fiona and Raymond in a permanent state of guilt. Fiona for not joining her sister at the party and Raymond for his failure to save his friend.

20

CONTINUES MUTE IN SPIRIT

I found it very difficult to keep silent about my discovery on Friday when I met Fiona and Raymond at the Book Barn to discuss rehearsal for the talent show. I knew them in a new light now. One that they didn't realize and I had no intention of revealing…at least for a while.

The pain they both must suffer from the poor decisions they made on that night was certainly enough to keep them wrapped in grief for a life time. I just wish they could realize neither of them were to blame for Daphne's actions that night.

I enjoyed the interaction between the two of them, though. If they could be birth siblings they couldn't have bantered more convincingly as brother and sister. Sometimes I believed them to be genuinely angry at one another, but then some unseen devotion arose to bond them in an eternal show of sincere love.

They shared a secret.

And I shared it with them, making me a weird sort of accessory to their pain.

When I told Fiona where I had been practicing and where I found my singing voice once again she nearly raised the roof with her squeal of excitement.

"Practice Room 3? At the high school? No way!" A mixture of delight and unabashed sorrow crossed her face so fleetingly I almost missed the confusion of emotions.

"That's where Daphne and I used to practice! How weird is that?"

So, I also shared a common ground with the sisters that I found comforting as well as disconcerting. That meant echoes of the White twins were imprinted on the cushioned walls of my secret oasis. Wow. Was our relationship that destined?

"Y'know, Daphne and I actually recorded a few things in there. I would love to revisit Room 3. There might be some sound track we recorded hidden away in there. Look around the next time you go."

I nodded in agreement, but inwardly cringed at the thought of disturbing the ghosts of days gone by. It kind of creeped me out that Daphne could still be living there, even in voice only.

I didn't believe in ghosts or unearthly spirits and I doubted Fiona did either. Her grounded belief in God and the Afterlife didn't quite correspond with the existence of ghosts and communing with the dead. I wondered what Pastor Hawkins would have to say on this matter.

Thinking about him brought a comforting warmth to the idea of Daphne and her celestial persona. I still had not brought myself to discuss this with him. I just didn't know how much he knew or how much he was inclined to discuss.

Since my life was becoming very, very interesting of late I should not have been surprised when my ride home from the Mall ended up being in Raymond's mini-Cooper. When we all left the Mall it was pouring the rain, far too violently for me to peddle home on my trusty bike. Fiona and I piled into the small vehicle as Raymond attached my bike to the rack on the back of his car.

Fiona's house was our first stop and she exited the passenger seat with a hurried wave of her hand before darting up the front steps. Even with the spring warmth in the air, the rain had settled a decidedly chilly feel on my skin. Raymond cranked up the defroster in the car and sat idling the motor until Fiona was safely inside her house.

What a gentleman.

I was just about to verbalize this thought when Raymond sighed deeply and took both of my damp hands in his own.

"Thank you for being such a good friend to Fi, Americka. She's been through some pretty tough times lately. You are just what she needed to bring her out of her funk."

I tried to settle my beating heart and to remind myself to breathe. I didn't know what was more disturbing. The fact his touch sent me into such a tizzy or his sincere generosity of kindness took precedence over any guilt or pain he felt himself.

He truly was a gentleman. I hoped my judgement of him was as accurate as it felt at that moment.

The rain diminished to a drizzle by the time we reached my house and the sun burst through the clouds as if God just rinsed the earth and was ready to bring spring back to us.

As Raymond removed my bicycle from the back of the car, Mom came out of the front door and waved us inside.

"I just took a fresh pan of brownies out of the oven. You are just in time for a snack." She didn't wait for us to reply but turned on her heels, leaving the door wide open and the invitation more of a demand.

"You don't have to come in if you need to go," I said. But I was encouraged by Mom's inclusion of Raymond into our home. Her moods were too difficult to read and I hoped inviting Raymond into the house was a step in the positive direction of healing. I just hoped I wouldn't need to verbally respond to any conversation that might unfold. I didn't think I could explain to Raymond my inability to talk in front of her.

I didn't need to worry too much about that, though. Mom did all the talking necessary once we three were settled around the kitchen island with a plate of brownies and individual glasses of milk. When she wasn't speaking, Andy entertained us to no end with his attempts to dunk a brownie into his own cup of milk.

Raymond was a natural with Andy and before he left I knew he was totally smitten with my baby brother. Not that it was too difficult to believe. Andy was quite adorable.

Mom got really excited when she found out about the talent show. There was a brief moment when I thought she expected me to respond to her question of why I had not mentioned it, but her excitement steered her toward more questions for Raymond.

"I have to be at the Book Barn early to open in the morning so I won't be able to pick you up, Meri. I hope it isn't raining so you don't get drenched on your ride in."

Mom's eyes shot in my direction so quickly I nearly dropped my glass of milk.

"Oh, no need to worry," said Mom, "I will be glad to bring Meri to the Mall. I need to do a little shopping anyway. This little guy," Mom tried unsuccessfully to wipe away Andy's milk mustache as she spoke, "is growing in leaps and bounds. I think he's due for a new wardrobe. Is that okay with you, Americka?"

I nodded in enthusiastic agreement, but I don't think she even noticed. Not only was Raymond smitten with my little brother, I think my mother was rather smitten with Raymond.

"You can just call me when you're ready to come home." Her second attempt at erasing the white mess from Andy's face was more successful.

"Oh, there's no need for that, Mrs. Miller. I'll see that Meri gets home okay. "

"How sweet of you, Raymond. Just give me a call if she's in the way of your work and I'll come by and get her."

Gee, thanks, Mom, for making me feel like an annoying kid in the way of more pressing business.

"Once, again, Mrs. Miller, no need to worry. Meri is not in the way."

Mom arched an eyebrow in my direction and I just knew that dinner conversation was going to be in the way of an inquisition into my love life.

And of that I wasn't too far astray. Later that evening, before we even sat down to eat, Mom was rattling on about the lack of "good" boys out there and how fortunate for me I had found one.

"What does Holly have to say about this boy? Does she approve of him?"

Before I could sort through her questions in my mind, the phone rang and I could tell by her tone Aunt Lydia was on the other end and my presence was no longer needed.

I had to grin to myself as I took my dinner plate to my room to finish. I had never fallen prey, like Holly and so many of the kids at school, to the belief my mother was clueless to the ways of youth, but I believe that she truly was clueless about this.

21

Diving In with Both Feet

Sure enough, my mother packed Andy and me into her car bright and early Saturday morning; she with a detailed list of Andy purchases and me with a vague list of whirling emotions about seeing Raymond and Fiona.

I wanted to be a friend to Fiona, but I was off-kilter about her feelings for Raymond and totally unsure whether or not to pursue my heart's guidance in the matter. Never having had a boyfriend and totally ignorant to the nuances of teen affections for the opposite sex, I was not prepared for this particular field of battle. Dad would not be happy with my lack of organization. A soldier needed to know her goals.

And I had no iota of an idea what mine were.

It didn't really matter, though, because Fiona had our day completely planned. Singing was only a portion of it.

"We need to look the part, guys. I think we need to dress accordingly, but I don't want to look too prissy-prissy. I know the song is churchy, but our church isn't one that abides by rules of dress. Y'know? But we don't want to look like a grunge band straight-out of the 1980s. Even with the Chris Tomlin twist, "Amazing Grace" is serious stuff."

Raymond and I both agreed with the need for visual appeal, but were at a loss how to accomplish Fiona's vision for us. Blue jeans and t-shirts were just a little too casual for such a big event while performing such an equally big song.

We set aside our wardrobe woes in lieu of playing around with Raymond's cardboard dulcimers. He attracted enough attention with his lesson fliers to start a class of beginners that would meet once a week after store hours. Mrs. White agreed to try this new venue out for the summer, so Raymond's late hours during the school week would not hinder academic endeavors. Not that he minded, though. Raymond didn't seem to require much sleep and his night owl instincts served to inspire his musical genius, if I was to believe Fiona.

I hadn't decided to be a part of Raymond's dulcimer movement, but after strumming for an hour or so, I thought it might be worth the effort if we were still speaking to one another after the talent show.

Fiona and I harmonized perfectly and I was beginning to feel really confident we could pull this off. We only had a little over a week to refine our performance and I forced the jitters to reside somewhere else in my brain.

"Of course, we need a dress rehearsal. Singing here with no formal audience won't do. So, I have taken it upon myself to arrange a debut." Fiona looked at us as if she just acquired a record label and we really had no choice but to agree.

"That's cool, Fi. Where?"

"Well, that's my big news." Fiona took an exaggerated breath and spread her arms wide before clasping her hands in front of her in the Yoga Namaste position that I had seen Mom and Aunt Lydia do the year they were determined to be self-taught gurus. "I spoke with Pastor and he has agreed to allow us to sing during Sunday service...drum roll please...tomorrow!"

The church was packed, absolutely packed.

I didn't want my mother to know about this, but Raymond made certain to inform her when he took me home from the Mall.

He impressed upon her the casual atmosphere of our congregation and the relaxed attitude of Sacred Sanctuary. He really seemed excited and promised a grand tour of the church campus.

Even though her inclusion in this test run of my new singing trio unsettled me, after giving it some thought, I realized this was something I secretly dreamed about. Getting Mom into a church setting, offering an opportunity for her to get things settled with God, maybe remembering a time when she had a need for Dad's beautiful Bible she kept locked away in a drawer until I requested it. I was new to the whole religion thing, but I felt like my journey was beginning smoothly.

I really liked the picture I had in my head of the three of us: Andy, Mom, and me, holding hands around the dinner table, heads bowed in sincere thanksgiving for what we were about to receive. It was very Norman Rockwell-ish.

I arrived at the church an entire hour before the first service, which probably showed on my sleepy face. A few minutes in the restroom with Fiona's skilled hands smoothed the linen wrinkles from my cheeks.

Even though she suggested to Pastor we sing at both services, she finally agreed the late hour would be the best since so many of the early morning congregates were of an older, more traditional, mindset. They preferred to use the dusty hymnal versions of what the praise team liked to amp up. I really thought our song was lovely enough to make a few conversions in that train of thought. Fiona was more familiar with the church, so I kept silent.

"Oh, man, it's a full house!" Raymond chortled from his perch at the sound table, making my stomach perform some rather uncomfortable somersaults.

"You girls are going to rock! And, to think, I knew you when." He smiled at me, just at me, and gave me thumbs up before returning to his duties as technical engineer of the church's sound system.

Fiona didn't seem to pay much attention to the growing audience in the sanctuary. Nothing seemed to rattle her when it came to public attention. She was as cool as the proverbial cucumber.

I scanned the sanctuary from behind the stage curtains for any sign of my mother. I saw Fiona's mother waving toward the back of the auditorium and my attention immediately flew to that direction. And there she was, my mother, in all of her finery. Even though

Raymond warned her of Sacred Sanctuary's non-dress code, Mom dug out her Sunday best, with a weird twist.

She wore the dress I had last seen at Dad's funeral. I knew she had a closet full of beautiful clothes, but she had chosen this one for today.

Maybe it had been the most assessable in her closet and while dealing with Andy she elected the easy way out. Maybe she hadn't even thought about what she was wearing. And, maybe, just maybe, I was over reacting.

So what that she wore the same dress I would always associate with the saddest day of our lives. My nerves were looking for any reason to back out of this performance. I knew that. My brain knew that. But my hands shook anyway and stage fright began to tighten the muscles in my throat.

While I was mentally analyzing my mother's wardrobe choice, I failed to see the entourage that came with her. Of course Andy was firmly glued to her hip, looking adorable in a miniature sailor suit complete with Popeye hat and a color-coordinated pacifier firmly in place. Not surprising, Lydia followed at Mom's heels, occasionally stopping to greet people she obviously knew from outside the church walls. Lydia was known as a social butterfly and she had a massive amount of connections. Being a former real estate broker guaranteed a healthy list of contacts, social and business.

I wasn't surprised to see Lydia trailing behind my mother, but the girl fidgeting at Lydia's side was a total, and not entirely welcome sight.

Holly continuously wiped her hand over her perfectly coiffed hair in a nervous attempt to straighten an errant strand. Holly was always mindful of her appearance, to the point of distraction. She, too, was dressed in her finest public display attire. I'm not certain Holly had ever been in a church before, so she had to rely upon her imagination for inspiration. And her imagination had gone crazy.

A mixture of classic 1960s chic, complete with a strand of pearls and pink suit, matching high heel pumps and complimentary matching clutch bag, Holly could have easily just walked off a movie set for a feature film about Jackie Kennedy. She looked lovely, perfectly put together and totally out of place.

I had no idea why she was here, but Mom evidently thought it a good idea to include my "best friend" in today's milestone. To make things worse and jar my nerves further, Mom caught me peeking from behind the curtain and started waving furiously as if this was a grade school play and she was with all the other mothers supporting their children. Not only did she wave, she grabbed Lydia's blouse sleeve and pointed repeatedly in my direction. Of course, Andy got in the picture when she lifted his little hand to wave at me as well. Holly looked completely mortified and for that I felt a little more akin with her presence.

"Wow, Meri, you have a fan club. A virtual crew of groupies," Fiona giggled behind me in an attempt to lift the awkward moment. "And they are a good-looking clan."

And they were. A bit overdone, but Mrs. White ushered them into her pew as if she expected them.

My suspicions were confirmed when Fiona continued in a hushed tone.

"I just thought it might be a good idea for your friend to see what you've been up to. Maybe she'll feel at home here and want to join our little church family."

I wanted to believe Fiona was sincere in her words but I could swear I detected a little smirk in her voice as well as on her face.

Was she trying to save the world one high school student at a time? I felt like we should concentrate on one soul right now and my mother was a good start.

The look of distaste and total discomfort on Holly's face was evidence enough she would take a lot of convincing.

With the parishioners safely in their seats and the lights adjusted to Pastor's liking, the service began with prayer, focusing on the widespread terrorist activity in our country and abroad. The events that led to Dad's death and a heightened alert in the area was of growing concern of late. The world was on alert and life was on cautious hold for many regions of the free world.

Pastor Hawkins's morning sermon focused on the strength of positive prayer and the importance of looking to the Master of supreme peace in these times of fear and distrust.

I found the sermon extremely disconcerting and not at all the positive reinforcement I needed with my questioning family and friends in the house. As I listened to Pastor's detailed description of the end of the world as we know it, I knew I would be pouring over the last book in my Bible later in the day. Hopefully I would find answers to the many questions that plagued my mind.

Why do people do things so destructive and mean? Why can we not all live in harmony? Why do images of terrorists always seem so incongruent with their purpose in life? They smile big, white-teeth smiles and mock us with undisclosed joy at ending innocent lives, all in the name of whatever guidance they were taught.

It was very difficult to be forgiving when all I could see in my mind was the aftermath of a relatively small bombing in my little town. Multiply that several times and I could not justify forgiveness.

Yet, Pastor Hawkins prayed for that very thing. I had a lot of praying to do myself.

Before I knew, it was time for Fiona and me to sing. I wasn't sure if all of my sermon analyzing distraction had been a good thing or not, but I wasn't nervous about singing anymore. In fact, singing seemed like the only thing to do right now.

Raymond played with the lights and the sound some as Fi and I positioned ourselves near the front of the stage. We decided that both our wardrobe and staging needed to be a casual blend of traditional and contemporary, so Fiona perched on a high stool with her guitar while I held a microphone slightly behind and to her side. The focus on her in the foreground was supposed to psychologically give me the idea she was the focus and not me. I was learning a lot more about public performance with Raymond's little tricks of the trade adding up in my brain. He seemed to think of everything.

We had taken some liberties with Chris Tomlin version of *"Amazing Grace"*, enough to make it ours without disturbing the perfect integrity of the song.

Fiona started strumming and humming softly in preparation for me to begin the actual singing.

I do not remember much about singing the song and I'm pretty certain I kept my eyes closed for the duration of my portion of the performance. As long as I was lost in my own little world, the thought of Practice Room 3 or the Book Barn, I was comfortable, floating, and having the best time of my life. I was afraid if I met the eyes of my mother, or Holly, or anyone in the audience my voice would forget to sing. And all I wanted to do at that moment was sing.

I sang for my family, for the sermon and Pastor Hawkins. I sang for Fiona and Raymond and even Daphne. I sang for all of the victims of extreme and inexplicable crime. I sang for heroes like my father.

And ultimately, I sang because I could.

Because Fiona and I were pretty much the service closure, following a brief benediction by Pastor, the room began to empty as Fiona continued to strum her guitar. I stood quietly in amazement at the reverent atmosphere in the room.

It didn't take long to tidy up the stage and gather our belongings. Fiona, Raymond, and I quickly met our assorted family members outside in the sunshine.

My mother, of course, was beside herself with praise and even Andy was particularly bouncy. I took him in my arms just as Raymond came to stand behind me in preparation for farewells.

"So, this is who is taking up all your time now, Meri. Introduce me to your new boyfriend." Holly's words were not laced with any trace of kindness. It was difficult to believe that after such a moving sermon anyone could still harbor negative thoughts. But there was Holly, giving it her best to usurp the hopeful feeling that surrounded me.

"Oh, and you talk to him, huh? Why don't you talk to me, Americka? I thought I was your friend. Your BEST FRIEND."

Fiona recognized the makings of a cat fight, not that I was a fighter, and quickly came to my rescue.

"Hi, you must be Holly. I have heard so much about you. Meri has nothing but nice things to say about her school friends and all the support they have offered her and her family."

Ouch! Fiona knew just how to ice a cake of sarcasm. The funny thing was Holly didn't even seem to recognize the caustic meaning of Fi's words. It was all about appearance and Holly would not allow herself to appear anything less than acceptable in the eyes of her public.

She needed to remain in charge of her public image and she seemed to realize sparring with Fiona was not in her best interests. Especially since Fi seemed to be offering her great words of praise.

Holly's entire persona softened and she intimately put an arm around my shoulders in a show of moral connection.

"I know. Poor, poor, Americka has been through a lot lately. We have been friends since we were little things, so she knows I WILL always be here for her. I just don't understand how that gorgeous voice can sing, but it doesn't speak anymore." Her hug was less than comforting and I didn't really feel any emotion in her touch.

Holly was playing a game and I didn't like it. I didn't know this Holly. She was not the childhood friend she professed to be. It was as if she had attended church and my public performance to be counted among the red carpet crowd. None of it meant anything more to her.

"Holly, I am just so glad to see you. Thank you for coming." My mother beamed in my direction as if she had pulled off the greatest feat ever. "Why don't you join us for Sunday brunch? I thought we could all go out for a Sunday treat."

Inside, I was vigorously shaking my head no, no, no. Today was too special for negativity and right now that is how I viewed Holly. Miss Negative. Miss Rain on my Parade. I just wanted to be with the people who wanted to be with me.

As if reading my mind, like I used to think she did, Holly said her goodbyes, anxious to remove herself from these unfamiliar and threatening surroundings. She probably wanted to get home to report to Janie and all of her online friends how horrible Meri behaved. I just nodded my head when she announced that she would see me in school tomorrow. I didn't really care and knew our paths would only cross in the hallway at class change. At one time, I would have worried about the status of our friendship, but for now I didn't really care.

Mom, Lydia, Raymond and the Whites decided to move our Sunday feelings to a local popular restaurant. It didn't bother me that Mom still believed I wasn't talking, mainly because I knew she wouldn't press the issue in public. Lydia kept giving me suspicious looks, but not to the point where I had any worries in that direction either.

I just wanted, no, needed to bask in the afterglow of what had happened this morning.

22

THE CALM BEFORE THE HOLLY STORM

I should not have been surprised at what I heard the next day at
school, but it hurt none the less. Because our lockers were right next
to one another, a scheme Holly and I managed to pull off for years,
overhearing any conversation Holly might have with Janie or anyone
else was not really a matter of eavesdropping. It just was what it
was. There was little chance for secrecy in such a limited area. But
the fact she didn't even attempt to conceal her words was something
that disappointed me.

Holly was a little over the top when it came to drawing attention
to herself, but I had never known her to blatantly be mean.

"Oh, you should have been there. It was more like a rock con-
cert than any church service I've ever been to." Holly nonchalantly
retrieved her text books for class, timing her next comments perfectly in an effect to draw in her listeners. "The music was loud, and
the minister, if that is what he truly is, wore blue jeans and his hair in
a ponytail. It was just…weird, even for Meri. I don't know what's
going on with her anymore."

"Wow, Holl, you don't think she's gotten herself involved in some
sort of cult or something, do you?"

I nearly chocked when Holly's response came out sounding like
this was *exactly* what she thought.

"OMG, that is so scary. A cult here in our town?"

"Poor Americka. She's been through some crazy stuff lately, hasn't
she? You need to talk to her, Holly. She will listen to you, won't she?"

I didn't recognize the voice posing the question and had to look up to identify the speaker. Holly had evidently been busy adding to her new fan base. I didn't know who the girl was, but she had obviously ingratiated herself into Holly's fold since she was busy organizing her possessions in what used to be Janie's locker. What was with that? Where was Janie?

"She doesn't talk to me at all any more. I was only at the church because her mother asked me, no, begged me to come. In fact, I don't think Mrs. Miller understands what's going on with Meri. She seemed awfully uncomfortable there, too." The actress in Holly was spot on with her pity act. She worked the crowd very convincingly. "I feel so sorry for her. She doesn't know what to do. I guess she was hoping that I could offer some advice."

This time my attempt to hide my presence on the other side of the locker wall caught the attention of Holly and her friends.

"Oh, there you are Meri. I wondered where you were."

Holly visibly played the part of a concerned pal, while her entourage busied themselves with looking busy in an attempt to cover the awkward atmosphere surrounding them. She brushed them off in a manner that suggested she would take care of this.

"I'll hook up with you guys at lunch," she said before placing her free arm in the crook of mine and chummily marching us to the first period of the day.

"Let's get to class, Meri. Don't want to be late, do we?"

She obviously did not expect a response and I don't think she would have heard if I had offered one. I didn't like this patronizing side of my former best friend. I had witnessed this ploy in the past and not been impressed. This girl had some serious issues of grandeur.

I let her lead me to class where she hovered over me as if I could not handle the day on my own.

Her behavior did not bother me, mainly because I knew for the remainder of the school day I could easily avoid any more contact. My goal was to get back to Practice Room 3 for some much needed privacy.

But today, Holly had other plans for me. She was totally determined to take me under her wing and nurse me back to what she felt was a normal existence. I don't know why she felt so threatened by my association with Sacred Sanctuary. Or if it was jealousy based on my relationship with Fiona and Raymond. Whatever the issue, Holly did not allow me to leave her sight at lunch time, insisting I sit at our old table and be a part of the mid-day gab fest.

The new girl in Holly's friendship circle was polite enough, but I knew her days were numbered, as much as Janie's had been.

Where was Janie? If I had any desire to participate in the lunch table talk I would have asked. But as it was, I had nothing in common with the words floating around me. So, I did what I was learning to do best—shut up and listen. And I'm glad I did.

That's when I learned Holly was currently lusting after Jake Planter, the school Jock of the Year. I hated to be so judgmental, but all of my dealings with school athletes tended to show a harvest short on intellect. Every once in a while, there emerged both brawn and brains under the same skin, but that was rare. And from what I knew of Jake Planter, my judgments were correct. And that probably suited Holly just fine. It was much easier to be numero uno when your plus one attracted more due to looks than to academic prowess. She could easily dominate a conversation while turning a few heads at the same time. Jake at her side was a bonus.

Evidently, New Girl was a recent transplant to our area. Of course, Holly would zone in on her. New Girl wore the latest designer labels and was absolutely breathtaking in appearance. She smelled great and spoke Holly's language, maybe too well. If she wasn't careful, Holly could easily loose her status as leading lady at Ellison High.

I couldn't believe how cynical I was becoming and I didn't really like this side of me. On the other hand, I was a little disturbed that maybe I had been just like Holly before I lost my dad and my voice.

"I'm sorry, but Meri doesn't speak. At least not yet, so I can translate for you."

I heard Holly before I realized what she was doing, right there in front of the entire student body. I couldn't help it. I burst out laughing and just couldn't seem to stop. The image of Holly performing some ridiculous gyration of interpreting a message from me was the most humiliating thing I had ever seen. Did she really believe that was the way to make her new friend understand me?

That was funny enough, but when I realized Holly was actually translating *for* me, my laughter took a radical turn into manic hysteria. *Why would I need a translator? I wasn't deaf.*

The new girl seemed to figure that out but not in time to save Holly from the mortal embarrassment that would haunt her until the end of the school year.

She looked ridiculous. More so than I at the moment.

She got what she wanted—attention.

Holly had a way of turning the ridiculous into positive PR and by the end of the day her antics were well received in the popularity polls. Everyone was talking about how she tried to make my condition more acceptable and her solid show of friendship more of a loyalty action than what it really was. Absurd.

I should have kept a better eye on her, though. By the time I got home that afternoon, my mother was beside herself with concerns about my friendship with an older college girl from a rock and roll cult religion.

"I knew she was too old for you, Americka. And your obsession with her church proves it even further. I forbid, absolutely forbid, you to continue any relationship with Fiona Whatshername and that fanatical organization she belongs to." Mother was literally wringing her hands while throwing any and every accusation via Holly my way.

"I mean, her family seems nice enough, but that girl is seriously disturbed and it is purely a result of untraditional parenting. The minister rides a motorcycle to his job. What kind of minister rides a Harley Davidson? It just isn't healthy, Meri. I know you have been under an enormous amount of stress. We all have, but your father would definitely not approve of this. Any of this. You are grounded until further notice."

Grounded?!

As far as I could remember I had never been grounded. And being grounded for worshipping God seemed like something out of medieval times. Since when had my family become so judgmental?

That was something my father would not approve of. That was one of the reasons he fought it out all those years in a third world country. Religious freedom meant everything to our nation. A nation my dad was more than honored to defend to the end of his days on earth.

I had to speak. I had to defend my rights as well as my friends.

But my mother was on a rampage and unwilling to listen to a word I might have uttered. At that moment I knew that I could talk, but she was not going to give me the opportunity.

Why and how she got her false information was a total mystery to me until I heard her mention her appreciation of Holly's voiced concern.

As soon as I shut the door to my bedroom, a first for me since we generally lived under the open door policy in my house, I booted up Ralph and went straight to the popular social media site where I knew Holly posted every little bit of important news, true or hearsay.

And there is was. An all-out campaign against cultist behavior in our town.

Sacred Sanctuary was under fire.

And it was all my fault.

23

PUTTING OUT THE FIRE AND BREAKING ALL THE RULES

My prison sentence put me in an uncomfortable position. The talent show was in five days and my sentence of home confinement was an entire month. There was no way that I would let Fiona and Raymond down. The talent show, what had once sounded as impossible as surviving the blast of a terrorist attack, was my goal right now. It was what steered my recovery from that awful day.

I just knew in my heart my father had put that public announcement in the mall right in front of Fiona as a reminder THAT life must go on and his daughter must sing. That was my "thing." That was my purpose in life. I had to sing.

Fiona, Raymond, and Sacred Sanctuary were all a part of this puzzle I had to solve. I really believed they were in my life for a purpose. And I believed everything happened for a purpose, a reason created by a higher Being. That higher Being was God and without all the pieces of this tragic puzzle I would never have realized that. My father didn't die in vain. He served his country and his family well while here on earth and now he was serving and guiding me from his new home in Heaven.

Okay, so call me a bit of a fanatic. That's now how I saw it.

My Mom wanted to blame Fiona and her church for horrible crimes and a path down the wrong avenue in life. I was trying to see it as a lifesaving adventure.

I just could not miss the talent show. And in not doing so I had to break a few rules in the Miller household. I had to lie. And I had to lie some more.

I read somewhere God forgives all sins at some point. I didn't want to bargain with Him. I don't think that was possible, anyway.

But I did want to pray for forgiveness and ask for guidance in this terrible mess I obviously created by becoming involved in His work.

Mom said nothing about curtailing my computer socialization while incarcerated so I had to take advantage of that until she realized the loophole in her punishment. Technology wasn't always a bad thing.

Ralph and I found Fiona's e-mail and I quickly shot out a carefully worded message. I didn't want her to take offense at the derogatory comments penned by Holly and I did not want her to think my mother was as judgmental as I thought she was right now. When she realized the goodness of Pastor Larry's teachings and the positive energy that attending Sacred Sanctuary provided she would feel horrible about grounding an innocent victim. I knew my mother, most of the time, and I knew she was not a bad person. She was just misled right now. Holly painted a convincing picture for a woman desperate to blame someone, anyone, for the pain she nursed daily.

I told Fiona all about Holly's public announcement on social media and about my mother's reaction to it. I wanted to recreate Holly's attempt at interpretation in the school cafeteria but figured that was mean. Since I was feeling rather righteous of late, I deleted that story for another time. It wasn't my purpose to make fun of Holly or join the ranks of the jury. I just needed Fiona's help in attending the talent show in the most honest way possible. Church activities were not going to be a viable reason for me to leave the house this week.

After writing to Fiona, I gathered my homework materials around me on the floor where I could work from my bean bag chair in comfort. As I reached for a wayward pencil under my bed my fingers touched an unfamiliar surface.

I pulled out my dad's personalized Bible. I traced his name embossed in gold paint on the cover and wondered about his relationship with God.

Our church attendance was sporadic and my parents never talked about religion, God, or anything remotely related to the subject. But somehow they were in possession of a lovely *personalized* Bible.

Who owned something like this if there was not a closer relationship to the reason for having it? You just didn't decide to purchase something like this and have it *personalized* if there was not a good solid reason. It was kind of like owning a Fender or a Gibson guitar but not being interested in playing a chord. There was a reason for owning that instrument, just as there was a reason for my father to possess this Bible.

Because any homework I had pending was actually not due until later in the week, I decided to put aside my normal straight-A mentality in favor of attacking this new mystery.

I had to laugh in spite of my recent misfortune. I had never pictured myself as the Nancy Drew type and yet here I was, surrounded by a growing list of detective assignments.

1. Daphne's death
2. Fiona's mysterious emotional ailments
3. My inability to speak in the presence of a select group of individuals
4. Raymond's involvement in Daphne's death
5. Raymond's romantic involvement with the White sisters

No, strike number five. That was irrelevant. I penciled it out, but left it visible on my notebook paper. It might come in handy later. For now I had three more mysteries to solve.

6. How to escape the house for rehearsal and the talent show
7. Why my dad owned this beautiful Bible, but never went to church
8. Why Holly had it out for me

I knew Lydia could, and probably would, help solve some of these mysteries. I just had to get to her before my mother colored the picture with her growing pessimism. Lydia was usually a rational, level-headed person, but she was also extremely loyal to my mother.

And I thought I could speak in front of Lydia. In fact, I think that already happened even if I had not exactly directed my words at her. It would be best to actually talk to her but if I dialed her phone number and no words came out she would get concerned and immediately call my mother or, even worse, come to the door. So, this had to work. I had to be able to verbalize my thoughts.

I checked at my bedroom door to determine my mother's where-abouts and was relieved to hear her preparing dinner and chattering to Andy as he observed from his high chair. If Lydia answered the phone quickly I had a few minutes to plead my case.

I gently returned my door to the closed position but left a crack in order to track my mother's movements. Oh, yes, I was becoming quite the detective. This might be fun after all.

After a careful impromptu run through of what I wanted to say to Lydia, I keyed in her cell phone number on my own phone. This was a novelty for me. I had never actually spoken on this phone. My only communication had been via texts. Strangely, I hadn't even thought about actually using it to *call* someone. Weird.

Lydia answered on the second ring. It probably took her a second to register the fact her pseudo-daughter, assumed mute, was calling her on the phone.

"Meri, sweetie, are you all right? Did you mean to actually *call* me or did you push the wrong button? If you did, just hang up and text me."

I couldn't let her hang up because she would alert my mother for sure.

"No, Aunt Lydia, I'm here." My voice felt and sounded raspy. A good decoy for Lydia to believe that my muteness had really existed all this time.

"I need your help."

After explaining my situation as thoroughly as possible in my self-inflicted time limit, Lydia was silent. Her silence was in thought, I hoped, and not furiously typing an email to my mother.

When Lydia agreed to my plan she became an accomplice in my crime. There was no going back.

I checked Ralph for any response from Fiona before going down to supper, but she was evidently busy with own after-school responsibilities. I would check again later, but for now I felt rather proud of my crimes. I think Dad would be proud as well.

I glanced at my father's Bible before sliding it once again beneath my bed. There would be time to look at it again before I went to bed.

I threw a silent prayer toward the heavens that Lydia would keep her promise and not alert my mom to our scheme.

24

FULL-FLEDGED FELON

Aunt Lydia was true to her word and picked me up promptly after school the next day. Mom totally fell for her friend's ploy of taking me out for a little restorative talk and dinner. I knew Mom trusted Lydia without reservation and I felt guilty for including Mom's best friend in my plan. But Lydia had semi-agreed that Mom was being unreasonable and was open to listen to my side of the story.

Lydia didn't question my request nor did she interrupt when I explained the importance of the task at hand. She did, however, warn me against the evils of lying to my own mother.

She also broached the subject of church and my friendship with Fiona.

"What do you really know about her, Meri? She is considerably older than you are and her family is, is…"

"I know. They are rich. Very rich. And we are not. But who cares? They are nice people. Remember, Mrs. White even came to the house during Dad's memorial." I didn't want to come off as too defensive, knowing Lydia was my last acceptable ally.

"It has just happened too suddenly, Meri. Your interest in attending church, the fact you won't talk to your mother, your friendship with this older girl. Your mother just doesn't understand any of it. She is still so engulfed in her grief that we need to walk on egg shells for a little longer."

So, we were supposed to treat Mom with kid gloves while the rest of us did what we could to move on with our lives. Seemed a bit foolish to me.

"Why don't you talk to your mother, Meri? She has to know your voice has returned. You two used to be so close."

But Mom didn't know my voice worked and for some reason I could not tell her that my selective muteness was most apparent when Mom was in the room. I didn't know why I couldn't talk to her. Or at least I didn't think I did.

"And why do you not talk to Holly anymore? You two have been as thick as thieves since as long as I can remember. And I know she really, really misses you. She has to."

I wanted to tell Lydia that was not true, but I didn't want to appear disrespectful.

"Does this have anything to do with that boy? Raymond?" I nearly fell over my own feet when she asked that question.

Why would any of this have anything to do with Raymond? He had nothing to do with this. Did he?

I promised Lydia I would explain everything over dinner after I rehearsed with my friends at the Book Barn. Lydia had some shopping to do and we decided to meet at the mall food court in an hour. Surely that would be long enough for me to create something plausible to tell her.

As it happened, though, rehearsal was secondary to the inquisition Fiona put me through as soon as she saw me enter the door to the Book Barn.

"What is going on, Meri? I got your e-mail, but didn't know exactly what to say, so I waited to see you in person. Are you in some sort of trouble? Tell me everything!"

And I did. I told her the entire painful truth of Holly's accusations and my mother's painful reaction.

The words spilled from my uncensored lips and I didn't bother to take stock of what might sincerely hurt my new friends. To be accused of belonging to a religious cult had to be hurtful.

But Raymond and Fiona listened with unconditional silence, offering an occasional murmur of condolence or surprised sigh of resignation.

"I am so, so sorry, Meri. Sacred Sanctuary has never held quite the reputation of what Holly wants to believe. Pastor Larry would probably think this is kind of funny if it weren't so sad. Does your mother think so poorly of us? Maybe I should call her or stop by and talk to her."

THAT was the last thing Fiona needed to do.

"No. No, that's not a good idea. Mom has some rather strange thoughts, but she really isn't in the mind-set to hear you out. Besides, I am not supposed to be here and if you did that she would know Lydia also lied to her."

"Oh, the wicked web created once we practice to deceive," Fiona chanted in a sing- song voice.

Raymond burst out laughing before replying. "I don't think that's how it goes, Fi, but we get your drift." He looked at me with pity and addressed the situation in his own way.

"What can we do for you, Meri? There has to be something we can do to change your mother's opinion of us or at least something we can do to change your so-called friend's behavior."

I found it funny that Raymond referred to Holly the same way Fiona had the day Holly stood me up.

"I just don't know guys. I *do* know the talent show is only days away and we haven't practiced a note today. I don't know how many times I can deceive my mother into thinking I am honoring my grounding while I'm really meeting you to prepare for a talent show I may not be able to make." My words hit me harder than I expected. Maybe I wouldn't make the show. Maybe this had all been for nothing.

"Well," Fiona began, "let's not think about the show right now. We sound pretty darn good without any more practice and it's more important to get you out of this mess and get Miss Holly to shut her ignorant mouth."

"Fiona! That is definitely not the Christian way to handle this," Raymond admonished.

"You know I'm not trying to be mean, Ray-Ray. I just do not understand why some people are like that. Even Daphne started thinking like that and look what happened to her. Why can't we just believe what we want to believe and everyone be happy with that?"

Both Raymond and I seemed to stop breathing at the mention of Daphne's name and for different reasons, I'm now sure.

Fiona didn't appear aware of the fact that she brought her deceased sister into the conversation. The tears that rolled freely down her face were evidence emotions were running high and she probably was speaking clearly for the first time in a long while.

"Fi, baby, what happened to Daphne has nothing to do with this. These are two totally unrelated situations and the big difference right now is that we can do something to help Meri. She is right here, right now, needing us to be strong and smart for her. Her mother is not a demon nor is she an illegal drug that rules anyone's life. She is a misguided soul in need of our help."

If I kept holding my breath I feared I would pass out right there on the overstuffed sofa in the Book Barn. Pieces to one of my puzzles were beginning to fit together and I did my best to keep silent so the mystery might come to completion.

"But, I should have been there, Raymond. I should have gone with her and made her realize what she was doing was wrong. Those people were not her friends. You knew that and I knew that, but Daphne was so drawn to them. I do not know why. She had everything she could ever want right in front of her. So why did she choose to throw it all away for the falseness they offered her?"

Fiona's tears began to fall in earnest and I hurriedly dug in my music bag for a wad of clean tissues to pass her way. For some reason I knew this was a big breakthrough for Fiona. It was as if she was just realizing her sister was no longer with her. Had Fiona really lived in such false illusion for over a year? Had she really, really believed Daphne was still alive?

I recalled all the references she had made about her twin since the awful day we met. Daphne was supposedly in the theater with Fiona watching a silly chick flick. Daphne and Fiona dressed in drastic opposition in order to claim a piece of separate identity and that is why Fiona's character was always a surprise.

Daphne was not at my father's memorial because she was working. Daphne was always busy working and picking up extra shifts because of some cute guy who had been hanging around the book store. Daphne and Fiona were never in the same place at the same time. Daphne's love life was the center of her life and she was boy crazy.

"Fiona, you cannot blame yourself for that night. Daphne made her own decisions based on what she wanted to do. If anyone is to blame it should be me."

And there you have it. Another wild-card twist in an already bazaar real-life crime story unfolding right in front of my eyes.

I handed Raymond another wad of crumpled, but usable tissues to staunch the flow of his own tears. The two of them didn't really seem to notice I was still there, so the least I could do was act as mediator. I was just relieved no customers walked in while this emotional storm was happening. I quietly moved toward the front door. I hoped I could secure the lock on the front door to waylay anyone who happened in.

Just as I was reaching for what I hoped was the lock, there appeared a beautiful face on the other side of the glass door. Mrs. White smiled at me in a quizzical fashion as she pushed the partially closed door open.

"Hello, Americka. It is so…"

Panicked, I signaled for her to stop talking. I didn't know what to do. Was it okay for her to witness Raymond and Fiona talking about her dead daughter? Was this something new or a repeat of the past?

When in doubt, do nothing. That is what my mother always said. But right now I felt like I had to do *something*.

So, I took Fiona's mother by the arm and guided her into the hall to a nearby stone bench. I glanced back at the store front to make sure that the door had secured itself. It may not be locked but at least it didn't look so inviting with a closed door. Maybe it was deterrent enough to allow Raymond and Fiona some quiet space to finally resolve their guilty feelings about the night Daphne died. Unfortunately, I was no longer there to hear all the missing pieces of the puzzle.

But here was another ally for my case. At least I hoped. Even though my mother was intent upon bringing down the entire family and the church, Mrs. White was a mother as well and they seemed to speak another language. The language of reason was a mother's second voice. Wasn't it?

I really, really wanted to hear what was going on in the Book Barn but I also needed all the help I could get in completing my goal of singing in the talent show on Saturday.

Aunt Lydia found me on the bench with Fiona's mother and if she made any decisions about the other woman's presence, she didn't comment. I felt badly for her.

Lydia was definitely thrown in the middle of a bad situation. Trying to be loyal to her friend and attempting to smooth waters with her friend's daughter. All the while grieving, in her own way, for our family. I said a little prayer that Lydia would see that the Whites were not bad people and that Sacred Sanctuary was exactly what its name professed. A sanctuary. A safe haven.

After placing a hesitant, but sincere peck on Mrs. White's perfectly sculpted cheek, I joined Lydia for more talking. I just knew my voice as well as my throat was going to ache by the time I hit the pillow tonight.

Talking was overrated, I decided.

But, by the time Lydia and I left Mrs. White, we had a plan.

25

THE BREAKDOWN OF A FRIENDSHIP

I was anxious to see Holly at school, but dreaded it at the same time. In all of our years as friends, I had never felt so indignant toward her. Not only had Holly avoided me during my time of need, she turned her back on any compassion I felt friendship required.

I didn't waste a second confronting her at our lockers. Janie was still a no-show in Hollyworld, but New Girl, whose name I still did not know, was joined at the hip. I practically had to physically pull them apart in order to gain Holly's attention.

"Good morning, Holly. Do you think we could have a little talk this morning?" I glanced at the new friend and added, probably rather rudely, but I didn't care. "Alone."

"Wow, Meri that was some greeting. You won't mind if Sabrina tags along. She knows all about you. I'm sorry you've never been formally introduced. Sabrina just transferred here from out west and I've been doing my best to introduce her to Ellison society. I think you two will get along just great. She's our new pal!" Holly flipped her hair across her shoulder in Holly-fashion.

"That's nice. Welcome to our high school, Sabrina. Now, I'm sure you understand Holly and I need a little privacy. We won't take long."

I stood my ground and made it clear this was a subject on which I refused to budge.

Without another word, I grabbed Holly around the upper arm and literally pulled her away from the lockers and an astonished Sabrina.

"Meri! That was just plain rude. What is wrong with you?"

While she attempted to disengage herself from my hold, I continued to pull her toward the ultimate meeting grounds of all high school coeds: the restroom.

"I'm sorry if you think I'm being rude, Holly, but this has nothing to do with her. She won't stray too far, I'm sure."

The girls' room door slammed behind us and even I was surprised at the force I used to corner my *pal* against a porcelain sink in the row against the wall.

There had been the occasional cat fight in this very bath room during my time at Ellison High, but it was never something I imagined myself participating in. Holly and I had actually spent some time giggling over girls getting physical, usually over something we viewed as trivial and not worth the time it took to receive a bloody nose.

"I need to know exactly what you think you're doing, Holly. Why did you post those horrible things on SM? You do know that my mother heard all about it and now believes I am running around with cult members and devil worshippers, don't you? Was that your intention? Why, Holly? Why would you do something so mean?"

I don't know who was trembling more, Holly or me. I had never been so outright mad at anyone in my life. Not only betrayed by her, but abandoned.

She seemed to get herself together faster than I did, though, and was ready with a comeback that was logical only in her mind.

"Oh, puh-lease, Americka, get a grip. Of course I didn't accuse anyone of worshipping Satan. That's ridiculous. But so is that whole church scene you threw at me. A preacher who rides a motorcycle? A church choir that sings rock-n-roll? One of the musicians was even playing an electric guitar!" She turned to face one of the wall mirrors and busied herself straightening her hair and checking her lip gloss.

"Does it matter what a person drives or what musical instruments make the music that fills a church, Holly? What do you even know about church music? I don't remember you ever stepping foot in a church unless your parents made you because it was fashionable to attend at Christmas." I worked hard to fight back the tears that threatened to ruin my indignation. Crying would not strengthen my words. "I just want you to stop publicizing all of this false information about something you know nothing about."

Holly didn't even blink. She continued to scrutinize her face for any signs of war wounds. I didn't have to lay a hand on her for her to make this situation fester. This was a Holly I didn't or want to know.

"Listen, *Meri*. I know you've been through a bad time lately, but you're making some very bad decisions. This girl, Fiona, is bad news. You do know that she and her sister are druggies and that boy they hang with is no better. I don't care what their last name is or who their parents are. They. Are. Not. Good. People. You are headed for trouble and if you're not careful you'll end up just like your dad. Dead."

If I was surprised by my own behavior earlier, what I did next came as the ultimate shock.

My arm was cocked back and my balled fist shot out so fast that neither of us saw it coming.

I hit her.

I hit Holly.

Right between the eyes.

"Earth to Meri. Earth to Meri."

I blinked once, twice, and once again. Holly stood right in front of me beside a smirking Sabrina. No evidence of being punched and no traces of indignation across her brow. We were at the lockers, not in what teachers refer to as the Porcelain Drama Department. No one was staring at us in astonishment. There were no administrators surrounding us in an attempt to break up the ensuing girl fight.

I had not hit Holly nor probably even said any of those hateful, but much deserved words to her. I had imagined the whole thing. A combination of relief and regret spiraled up my spine.

"Americka, you just kind of zoned out on us, girl. I was just introducing you to Sabrina and you went away somewhere." The lilt in Holly's voice confirmed that she found this behavior an affirmation of my recent bizarre antics. I am sure she was mentally patting herself on the back about being so very correct in her assumptions that poor

Americka was losing her mind. "You need to get it together, my friend. Maybe stay away from those new friends of yours."

Holly completed her inspection of her morning make up in the little mirror hanging in her locker and adjusted the weight of her text books to accommodate the imposing leather backpack she took everywhere.

Why she just didn't put the books in the bag had always been beyond me. I used to think she enjoyed lugging all that around until she confessed that if she looked overwhelmed with "baggage" guys were likely to offer assistance. Another attention-getting ploy by Holly. Why had it taken me so long to realize her true colors?

"Anyway, I would say we'll save you a seat at lunch, but I know you have better things to do, so I won't bother. You'll know where we are if you decide you join us. Tootles!"

And with a little finger wave, Holly and Sabrina floated down the hall enjoying some secret giggle, probably at my expense.

Great. I had every opportunity to let Holly know how I felt and my inability to voice any of that just drifted off into thin air. Holly was going to win this battle and I was doing nothing to prevent it.

I was still shaken at my morning behavior when I returned home at the end of the school day. I could not ever remember being so mad at someone and so willing to revert to physical violence in order to prove my point. I guess I was grateful I had imagined the whole thing.

But that did not lessen the anger I felt toward Holly's irrational treatment of something she knew nothing about. How dare she insult Pastor Larry and his church in such a public manner? Social media was in the news a lot these days, being the scapegoat of all sorts of illegal and immoral behavior. There was no way to place blame on the computer that published such rubbish. The blame was solely the fault of the typist and Holly was fully armed.

I didn't want to get in a cyber war, but for some reason I felt Holly would most likely pay more attention to online arguments than any face-to-face combat I threw at her.

I booted up Ralph and reluctantly logged on to Holly's personal SM page. Finding the expected barrage of selfies taken from her cell phone I didn't take any time smiling over her silly film antics. What once would have entertained me now just filled me with disgust. Why she needed to post every little aspect of her life baffled me. But at least those personal snippets were nothing in comparison to the barrage of hate messages she posted against Sacred Sanctuary and its congregation. I was totally ashamed of her and humiliated for the good people who patronized the church. They had done nothing to deserve the wrath she painted around an otherwise peaceful place of refuge.

It didn't take long to find snap shots of me performing my solo on Sunday. I wasn't interested how photogenic I looked, but I needed to see for myself what kind of destruction she had photo-bombed around me. And sure enough, there it was. How she had done it I didn't know, but there on the stage was a superimposed image of a crude pentagram where the lovely gold polished cross should have been.

So she was really serious about this cult thing. I didn't want to feel concerned, but my heart and my mind suddenly reached out to my former friend. Was she so starved for attention that she would stoop to such horrible tactics?

I didn't know anything about cultist behavior other than anything that had wormed its way into prime-time television. And of course that couldn't be believed. It was so Hollywood.

The last thing I wanted to do to Ralph was insult his wiring with research of something so vile. So I didn't go that route. As I pondered my next play in this bazaar game of good and evil, my eyes fell to the cover of the soft moleskin Bible that peeked out from under the edge of my bed skirt.

I hurriedly fell to the floor to claim it and scoop up my dad's tome as well. I hadn't spent much time, if any lately, reading from this beautiful gift from Sacred Sanctuary. And I had forgotten my intent to search through my dad's Bible in hopes of piecing together more of his church relationship puzzle.

No time like the present. Pentagrams and Satan worshippers could wait. I think maybe claiming the positive was a better plan anyway.

I opened my Bible first but it didn't take long for me to realize I didn't even know what I was looking for. There was an index at the back, but it was rather vague and definitely not detailed enough for my already ignorant Bible-brain.

I needed something more substantial for my arguing defense.

Ralph tinged on my desk to alert me of a new e-mail, but I just waved at him to indicate I could not be distracted at the moment.

That was when I realized I might seriously be losing my mind. Interacting with a computer as if he/it were human. Maybe Holly was right about me.

My dad's Bible was a little bigger than mine and I couldn't be certain if that was because it held larger print or more content. The only way to know was to crack open the spine and dig in.

That's when I discovered the enormous amount of reference material included in this work of prose, poetry and basic life lessons. This was like holding an entire college degree in my hands. No wonder scholars spent so much time and money in research and study concerning this single bound volume.

I found something called a concourse at the back of Dad's Bible and this is where my research truly began.

The concourse cross-referenced according to scripture number and topic. This was exactly what I needed. There was a treasure trove of information right at my finger tips and before long I was so engrossed I missed supper, forgot about Holly's hate posts and didn't even brush my teeth to ready for bed. When my alarm sounded bright and early Tuesday morning, I woke clutching Dad's Bible to my chest, sore from sleeping on the floor.

I had to hurry to get ready for school, but the rushed preparation was worth it. And I thought Holly could dish out the hateful emotions. Whoa, was I ever mistaken. I didn't even touch the bulk of this Holy work and I knew the delicate pages of the Bible were jam packed with blood, gore, hatred, disappointments and the most precious words ever written.

My dear Holly was definitely out of her league.

26

"Your Word Is A Lamp Unto My Feet And A Light Unto My Path"—*Psalms 119:105*

It took some quick moving and clear thinking to pull off what I did to Holly's locker. But I did it.

For some reason this scripture stuck in my head and I knew it provided a good "come back" to Holly's poor choice of SM words. That is if she gave it some serious thought.

Initially I planned to eliminate the Bible verse reference, but then I realized she needed to know this came from an accountable source. Since she was such an expert on church policy, I felt she could not possibly refute the validity of my defense.

Even though I wanted to stick around and see her reaction, I also needed to be out of sight, out of mind for now. I'm sure she could figure out who taped the handwritten banner to her locker, but a confrontation was not something I wanted to undertake this morning.

I still needed to get back to Mrs. White concerning my plan to make it to one more rehearsal session without the wrath of my mother ruining that for me. I knew I couldn't mention the White family in conjunction with any reason to break the conditions of my grounding, but at least I had a legitimate destination if my mother agreed to let me out of the house this evening.

Since academics came first, I assumed this rule applied even during imprisonment. So, the research project I was assigned suddenly became an urgent task that required more information than Ralph could provide. I needed access to a printing machine, copies of library-stored microfiche film, and colorful display items.

I knew I was stretching the truth way-far out of context and the result of this deception was certain to be a life sentence of home confinement, but I had to do this. I had to prove something to my mother, to Holly and to myself. Somehow, my Dad was involved as well. My dreams were taking over most of my night hours and he even crept into my day-time musings.

I couldn't find any underlying theme to his visits other than the simple message to "sing." And if that was the answer my father, living or deceased, was sending me that was the message I would honor.

My day progressed with little fanfare and I didn't hear from Holly, not even a little wave of the hand in the hallway. I didn't really care. I knew any reaction to my posted scripture lesson would be on line and not of the more personal manner.

My biggest concern was to get to the Book Barn without being seen. When Mom learned I really needed to go to the public library and my reason was legit, she didn't have any arguments.

I DID feel guilty for deceiving her. And I hoped God would see fit to overlook this sin.

I made it to the Book Barn as quickly as my two-wheeled steed could be pedaled and was met with a great deal of sympathetic enthusiasm from Fiona and Raymond. Mrs. White was manning the register and offered a slight smile of resignation. I knew she didn't really approve of my tactics, but she also wanted to encourage my spiritual growth. I had a way of putting people in contradictory situations. I imagined that was a serious sin, too.

Fiona, Raymond, and I were satisfied with what we decided would be our dress rehearsal for Saturday even though there were three days between now and the actual performance. They didn't want to put me at risk for any further punishment and we all hoped my mother would loosen the chains in time to allow me to go to the mall on Saturday. We all agreed as long as I mentioned Holly in my Saturday plan, Mom would be more receptive to an outing.

As soon as we finished our impromptu rehearsal, I hugged my friends, Mrs. White included, and promised to be in touch. They were going to include Pastor Larry in our plans and that reassurance of a spiritual guide on board made me feel a little better. I knew he and I would be having a long talk in the hopefully not too distant future. My family needed to come together under the umbrella of his comfort.

Mom didn't ask too many questions when I returned home although I was ready with an earnest answer to any of her inquiries.

As of yet, she had not demanded any actual verbal explanations from me, still content to believe my voice was working fine.

I was actually beginning to believe that I could continue this charade for some time. Mom's state of mind was still too fragile to force me into any type of speaking commitment. Made me wonder whose mental stability was really at stake here.

Just as I had assumed, when I logged on to Holly's media page that evening, it was full of raving agreement with the mysterious leaver of Bible scripture on her locker. She was all over the sentiment I left and in full agreement that scripture was the best armor with which to fight the cult invasion of Ellison.

She had even attempted to quote her own Bible verses in response to my own. Happily surprised with the time she spent in research of scriptural reinforcement, I was also surprised Holly was in possession of a Bible of her own. Of course, she could Google anything and didn't really need an actual Bible to quote what she did.

I didn't bother to add any dialogue to the conversation she had opened with other on-line participants. I was afraid my identity would be too easy to trace, even with the use of an alias user name. So, I just let what I had already done continue to sink in. Maybe tomorrow I would attempt to approach Holly again. This time without the inconvenient "zoning out."

My mother had always said "kill 'em with kindness" is the best rule of thumb.

Before I readied for bed that night, I was confronted with probably the most unexpected surprise I could never imagine.

Mom came to my room to ask me about the whereabouts of Dad's Bible. She appeared surprised, though, when I scooped it off the floor where I had left it after my sleep over with it.

What she had in mind, though, was much bigger in scope.

"Americka, I've been doing some thinking and I have decided it is time for our family to join a church. A church that reflects all the morals and standards I want you to embrace." She took a moment to clear her throat and maybe let this news settle in.

"Your father and I never really adopted a religious life after you were born. Your grandparents, on both sides, were social church goers, and we used to attend Sunday services with them. Of course, I always felt like it was more an act of public show than for any real reason of devotion. With the current state of your relationship to a church influence, I think it's time to show you what going to church really means."

Mom looked down at the Bible in her arms. She had been grasping it as if for strength of some kind. "Your father certainly loved this old thing. It has seen as much of war as he did."

For a moment Mom's face softened and I saw a glimpse of my mother before Dad died.

It didn't last long, though.

"So, we will be attending morning services at Grace Presbyterian this Sunday. That is the church Holly and her parents attend. Having her there should make you feel more at ease and hopefully she can help you become more comfortable with a more *conventional* way to worship God."

Whether Mom really believed what she was saying or if this was a ploy to bring Holly and me back into the folds of a more acceptable routine I didn't know. At one time, I would have been thrilled to be a part of Holly's spiritual life. But knowing what I did now about my old friend, I was skeptical about the whole situation.

Holly had never mentioned going to church. In fact, it was her routine, and my old one as well, to sleep in on Sundays before getting together to plan our weekly wardrobes and social schedule. This smelled rather rotten to me, but as long as it diverted Mom's attention from the darker side of my interests, I could do nothing more than to go along with her.

"Oh, and I met with the minister there earlier today. He seems to think it would be in our best interests to come to the church Saturday afternoon for a little meeting. I agree we should use that time to orient ourselves to the overall functioning of the church. So, we will leave here around 11:00 on Saturday. After our meeting with Reverend Hawkins, I will treat us to lunch at the Mall. Make sure your homework is finished and all of your school responsibilities are tied up before that."

My mouth worked furiously to form words of protest, but she was gone before the first syllable escaped my lips.

This can't be happening! The talent show was at 1:00 on Saturday! At the Mall!

Those famous words about webs of lies echoed in my brain. It was becoming a habit.

"By the way, Meri," Mom had reappeared at my doorway just as I felt the hateful blur of tears forming in my eyes. "I know you have something a little more presentable to wear on Sunday than what you wore the last time you attended…church. Make sure you select a proper dress for Sunday. Grace Presbyterian is *not* something as silly as the church of Go. Grace is a respectable place of worship."

Her footsteps could still be heard on the wooden floor of the hallway as I flung myself dramatically across my bed and allowed myself a good old fashioned pity party.

I didn't go down to the kitchen for supper for the second night in a row. I just could not face my mother, even though I missed Andy's sweet face tremendously. The gurgle of my empty stomach reminded me of the skipped meal, but my pride would have to provide sustenance for now.

I knew Fiona would be available via phone, text or e-mail. It wasn't worth the risk to be heard talking on the phone. So far, Mom hadn't remembered to take away that privilege as part of my punishment. E-mail was easier to cover up in the event she came back to my room. As long as I was hanging out with Ralph, I could disguise my real actions as working on my research project.

I fired out a lengthy e-mail to Fiona, describing this new twist in my increasingly twisted life. I knew she would reply with the appropriately sympathetic words I needed to hear right now. In fact, I trusted her to come to my aid.

What she did reply with was totally unexpected, but Fiona-brilliant.

Evidently, Grace Presbyterian was a very familiar territory for Fiona and her family.

"I practically grew up in that church, Americka," she wrote. "My parents and their parents and their parents before them were all longstanding members. It is a wonderful place. But when Reverend Hall moved into his position there, some rather strange politics evolved that even my grandparents are still adjusting to. It is still a great place, very classy. Mom wasn't real happy at first when Daphne and I discovered the music program at Sacred Sanctuary, but after being shamed into attending a service or two she was sold. And with her parents' blessing. My grandfather firmly believes it isn't the sign above the door that is important, but the people and the emotions inside that are. They even come to our special church programs when Daphne and I perform."

It was the first time in a while that Fiona referred to her sister in the present form and I hoped she wasn't reverting back to the desperate girl she was beginning to leave behind in the name of reality. But her next sentence solidified her successful road to recovery.

"I think Daphne would want me to go back there for another service. So, that is what I will do. On Sunday my mother and I will be there as well. That'll show that little Holly doll what a Satan worshipper I am, won't it?"

I could hear Fiona cracking herself up even without the benefit of an audio to accompany her words.

"But we have to get you out of this meeting on Saturday. Or at least shorten it. I don't know Reverend Hall very well, but Mother does. I would ask her what to do, but we agreed not to involve any more innocent victims than possible, so let me think on this overnight. It will all be okay, Meri. Just believe that it will."

And with that, Fiona and I signed off, with her sounding much more confident than I felt.

I didn't read my Bible that night nor did I go to bed without completing my normal toiletry routine. That is probably why my dad decided to visit me in my dreams again. Clean breath was a much more pleasant way to speak with one another, even in dream mode.

This time we were not on the battlefield nor in the musty dorm room, but we were at the altar of the most beautiful church I could imagine. There were baskets of freshly cut roses surrounding us and the candle light from the pulpit cast a soothing glow on the dimly lit room. There was no one else in the sanctuary, but the decor indicated something very special was about to occur.

When I awoke in my quiet little bedroom, I still felt the calm with which the scene in the imagined church filled me. Whatever the reason behind my dream, I felt good. I felt refreshed and my anxiety level was manageable.

Today was a new day and nothing would go wrong unless I allowed it.

"Wow, thanks, Dad," I whispered into my pillow. I refused to doubt him. He was my dad.

27

HOLLY, HOLLY, HOLLY

If I didn't know any better I would swear Salem had come to Ellison and the witch hunt was on. It was Holly's turn to get to school early and her decorating skills were without a doubt at their best.

As I walked down the locker-filled hallway toward my own, I knew that what looked rather uniform now would be a littered mess by the end of the day. On every olive-green locker door was a large unlined notecard anchored perfectly in the center of each door. Now *that* had taken some time. Who knew how Holly had pulled this off or how many hands she had employed to assist in the task? At first I thought this was something accomplished by the student council in preparation for next year's officer elections, but even the student council didn't take such pains to stage an event.

I slowed my pace before entering my own bank of lockers to inspect the message neatly typed on one of the cards.

"Repent and Be Blessed."

There was no scripture identification added, so it was more than likely Holly just inserted her own thoughts to claim as gospel.

As far as I could tell, each card held the same message so there was no attempt to spread knowledge other than this cryptic statement.

There was such a conflict about religious content in the public schools that it would not surprise me in the least if the administration wouldn't hop right on the bandwagon to discover the individual or individuals behind this brazen violation of school code.

Of course there was no direct relationship between church and state in the message, but social media ran the school, the town, the nation. So one would have to literally be a slug to not be aware of Ellison's latest hot gossip.

There was a witch in town. And she belonged to a major cult disguised as a well-established place of worship. Wow, how had this remained hidden for so long only now to be discovered by a high school junior who was so wrapped up in drawing attention to herself that Sacred Sanctuary had been on the back burner until she adopted it as her own? I guess when I thought about it that way; Holly really did have a major project on her hands. Good for her.

Surrounding my own locker area was a large group of my classmates and a few gawking underclassmen as well. There was not a senior in sight. They had better things to think about since their days were numbered. In two weeks they would officially be graduates. School drama was beneath them.

Lucky seniors.

At first I figured Holly was just holding court until bell time, but the closer I got, the bigger my dread grew. Yes, my old friend was there, but the attention was less on her and more on the makeshift shrine erected in the center of the hallway.

A sweet, smoky smell attacked my nostrils as I got closer and I knew the smoke alarm must need new batteries if it wasn't screeching in protest. A thin stream of smoke trailed from the incense burner to the ceiling in the precise direction of said alarm.

I didn't know if this was an exorcism or an ancient religious ceremony. I did know Holly had really gone overboard. The note cards were one thing…harmless really. But burning anything in school, incense included, was a serious violation and there would be repercussions. This was seriously scary.

Quickly evaluating my morning schedule, I realized I didn't need to go to my locker this morning. I could avoid this entire debacle and not be counted as one of the participants. If I circled around in the opposite direction, my path would take me out of the way for my first class, but it was worth it to not be counted as one of Holly's warriors. This was her fight. She created it. Not me.

My decision to lay low felt right and it seemed to work until midway through second period. As we were busily scribbling notes in preparation for next week's final exam, the distinctive squeak of the intercom announced our school secretary's introduction to a message from the office.

In my three years at Ellison High, Miss Helen had never gotten the hang of the mechanics of the intercom. What had first alarmed me as a freshman was now an event of comic relief. But the message was anything but funny when my name was part of the office request.

"Americka Miller, report to the office. Americka Miller, to the office."

Of course all eyes flew to my seated direction in the back of the class and Mademoiselle nodded her approval. The orderly note-taking session would not be the same, though. All interest was set on me and not the history of our country. Hushed whispers circulated around the room and even a few nervous giggles accompanied me on my slow walk to the door.

I was not alone in the office waiting area. Already seated and expertly twisting her blond hair around a painted finger nail was Holly, smirking as if with some huge secret. Instinct told me to ignore her but survival insisted I rise to the occasion.

"What's going on?" I asked her softly.

She actually looked shocked that I could have such a stupid question on this, her day of resurrection.

Her painted lips (they matched her nail polish) parted as if in reply when the principal's office door opened and Miss Helen directed us to the enter sanctum.

The principal's office. The place no one wished to visit, as it surely meant punishment of some kind.

I always thought that was funny, and not of the ha-ha variety. In elementary school during spelling class, our teacher helped us distinguish the difference between the words *principle* and *principal* by reminding us that our *principal* would always be our *pal*.

I guess that worked for spelling purposes, but right now I wasn't so sure that the spelling lesson was as accurate as it seemed then.

The issue became even less funny when the first person I saw in the inner office was my mother. I could add this to my growing list of mysteries, but I figured her presence would be cleared up in short time.

"Oh, Americka," My mother sobbed as dignified as possible while moving Andy from one side of her lap to the other. "What is going on?"

I wanted to know the answer to her question as much as she. We were both in the dark on this one.

"Good morning, Americka," Principal Jones did not rise from her throne, but at least had a greeting for me. "Thank you for joining us."

As if I had a choice, I thought.

"It has been brought to my attention, thanks to Miss Woods, that you might be involved in some rather disturbing extracurricular activity. I felt this needs to be 'nipped in the bud,' so to speak, with as much expediency as possible."

I dared to glance over at Holly who elected to cower in the seat closest to the exit as if her time in the interrogation was likely to be brief. Or was it the coward's way of joining her own party?

She kept her eyes solidly on Miss Jones and I could see by her expression she was exactly where she wanted to be. What a snake in the grass.

"Would you like to explain your actions of this morning, Miss Miller?" The formality of Miss Jones's tone clearly set the mood for all of us in the room. This was no longer the space of a princi*pal.* This was clearly an official disciplinary visit.

I had to find my voice. I must say something.

"I'm sure Americka had nothing to do with this, Miss Jones. As I explained on the phone, Meri has a distinct aversion to fire. She would *never* be involved in anything involving arson."

Whoa. Hold the door. Fire? Arson? What had I missed?

Holly didn't move a muscle, but my mother's crying became a bit more urgent. I did NOT want my mother involved in this.

"And as I described to you on the phone, Mrs. Miller, even though Americka was not present when the fire was discovered, witnesses affirmed it was her locker that was filled with this incense ingredient that caused the actual fire. Thank goodness it was found early enough and was of an innocent enough nature that evacuation was not necessary. We did find it rather suspect your daughter was not available to comply with my initial request she come to the office. We need to investigate her whereabouts at that time."

With that, Miss Jones's gaze fell directly on me.

"Where were you between the times you entered school this morning and the first period bell, Americka?"

Oh, no. My decision to visit Practice Room 3 prior to the beginning of the school day evidently wasn't the best place to avoid all the hoopla in the locker hall this morning. And all in the name of staying out of trouble. Sheesh. I had played right into Holly's plan. She evidently had started a fire, on accident I sincerely hoped, and left it for me to clean up. Literally.

So the incense ceremony hadn't been in the middle of the hall as I had first assumed. She had lit the foul smelling stuff in my locker to exorcise demons? Wow, she was really misled.

I squirmed a little bit in my seat, not because I was guilty but because I could not trust my voice to make its public debut in time to save me.

A knock on the slightly opened office door prevented me from total panic.

"Excuse me, Miss Jones, may I join this meeting for a moment? I may be able to offer some argument for the defense."

Mademoiselle Elise Bouffant, arguably the physically most beautiful woman on the face of the earth, or at least at Ellison High School, had been an enigma since her first day on staff at the high school. Her exotic appearance and musical French accent had immediately enamored the male population and her sincere concern for her students made the females comfortable in her presence. I had been fortunate to have her for class all three years of my stay here.

She was a busy instructor, providing the French curriculum for three levels of that language and teaching junior American Studies, the class from which I had been dismissed to come to the office.

"Forgive me for overhearing your question for Americka, but I believe that I can help with the answers."

My ears perked up at this unexpected referee and I hoped the ears of everyone else in the room reacted in the same manner.

"I do not believe Americka was any place near her locker this morning. When I entered the building this morning I was concerned about the meeting of students in the junior hallway. I usually take a short cut through that hallway to get to my classroom when I am running a bit late." Mademoiselle blushed slightly at her admission of tardiness. "The hallway was very congested, so I elected to detour through the music wing. In fact, I followed Americka, who apparently wanted to avoid the traffic as well. I assumed that Americka remembered that all she needed for my class this morning was her notebook and writing utensil, because she normally is armed with all of her text books when she comes to class." Mademoiselle directed her white, white smile at me, and I know I probably glowed in the light of those pearly enamels. She just had that effect on people.

"I have been aware for some time Americka spends as much of her free time as possible in that music room, so there didn't seem to be anything suspect about her behavior. Everyone needs a quiet place in which to reflect, don't they Americka?" Her eyes had not left my face the entire time she spoke about and to me. For some reason I knew she knew exactly what I had been doing in Practice Room 3.

"So, the point of my interruption," Mademoiselle returned her attention to Principal Jones, while expertly including everyone else in her public speaking stance. "Is to make certain Mademoiselle Americka is not included in any punishment involved in this morning's fire drill. She couldn't have heard the alarm. Those music rooms are sound proof and do not allow outside sounds to penetrate. Which is something I believe we need to investigate further. I am surprised the state fire marshal has not called us on that violation all ready."

These final words were directed toward our good principal, turning a disciplinary action into a more serious matter of public safety.

Miss Jones nervously shuffled some papers on her desk. Holly notably choked a bit on the forbidden chewing gum she had been hiding in her cheek. My mother looked slightly relieved and Andy clapped. Yep, my brother was smitten with the French charms of my teacher. What a typical guy. All male, that's my Andy.

"Ooo la, la, Mon Cheri. So adorable. May I?" the beautiful woman held her hands out to Andy with a questioning expression toward my mother who immediately relinquished her hold on my brother. Of course this exquisite woman could hold her precious baby. Under the spell of French charms, there was no reason not to comply with her request.

As my teacher got cozy with Andy, Miss Jones attempted to bring order to this turn of events. The control of the entire meeting had suddenly left her hands.

"Well, I guess an apology is in order, Americka. We, I, will personally see to it those music rooms are updated with the newest smoke and fire alarm features. And I am sorry about the contents of your locker. It was a total loss. I hope there was nothing of much value in there."

Sure, just all of my notes and text books from this semester. Final exams were going to be interesting.

"Take this note to your next class, Americka. Your teacher will be made aware of the circumstances that surround your absence of class materials. I am so sorry to bring you down here, Mrs. Miller. Trust me when I tell you that Americka is an exceptional student. I am personally relieved she was not involved in this mess. Thank you for coming. Americka, you may go to class."

Holly jumped up to lead the way out the door, but came to an abrupt halt with Miss Jones's next words.

"Not you, Miss Woods. You will remain with me."

I hugged my mother before leaving the office, but I didn't' get the chance to do the same with Andy. He was totally in love. The last thing I heard as I drifted down the hall was the shared cooing noises from my teacher and her latest fan.

28

Bombs Bursting In Air

Mom went overboard for the rest of the week, making it up to me. She was still suspicious of Fiona and Sacred Sanctuary and she was baffled at Holly's involvement in this cult situation.

"Why would she do something like this, Meri? She's your friend."

Yeah, Mom, I know. My dear, dear friend. She lit my locker on fire in an attempt to exorcise demons. All in a show of friendship. Yep. Pinky swear and all that.

My grounding was lifted slightly and my sentence would terminate at the end of the week. I was grateful Fiona and Raymond had agreed we were good to go for the talent show on Saturday. Because Mom was still adamant about the church thing this weekend, I was still obligated to attend the meeting at our "new" church. Fiona promised she had a plan and I had to trust her ability to make things okay. She had a way of doing that.

"Are you going to be okay without all of your notes? Americka, I am so sorry your things were destroyed in your locker, but it could have been much, much worse. You could have been...well, I am just happy the fire alarms are going to be installed in those practice rooms. Who ever heard of such a thing? The Board of Education could be liable for horrible...I'm just glad that this will be resolved."

Mom did her best to not mention death, but I could read between the lines.

I wanted to assure her my academic future was still intact. The one notebook that held all the wealth of EHS instruction was safe. I kept all my notes between the covers of one notebook and that notebook was always with me. I hated that the expensive textbooks were lost but I could not think of one important item in my locker I would miss.

At one time, I would have been devastated at the thought that notes and silly gifts between Holly and me were gone forever. Not now. Not with the knowledge of how disturbed my friend was. What was she thinking?

So, bright and early Saturday morning, I logged on to Ralph with my fingers crossed that today's events would unfold with little conflict and what had started out as a fun enterprise with my new friend, Fiona and newer friend Raymond, would end with as little fanfare as possible.

I had no idea how I was going to pull it off, but I instructed myself to tell no more lies. I would deal with my mother's reaction to the talent show when the hour struck 1:00. We should be at the mall before then for our Saturday after-meeting-the-new-minister lunch. Granted, it would be very difficult to avoid the talent show hoopla with it being center court in the mall, but I would worry about that later. The plan was to meet Fiona and Raymond at the Book Barn, so we could make the short walk to the concourse together.

I found an e-mail from Fiona assuring me that today would be remarkable and not to be nervous. I could easily hear her voice in my head and wondered if she was as unaffected by the enormity of my deceit as she let on. Just as I was logging off the computer, my cell phone alerted me to a text.

See you in a few.

I guess Fiona had not looked at the time. "In a few" to me meant shortly, in a few minutes. Fiona and I would not see one another for a few *hours*. She must be more nervous than I thought.

Andy had already drooled the contents of his sippy cup on the front of his sailor shirt, so I hurried to wipe it clean before Mom insisted on a complete wardrobe change. I knew from experience that could take more time than I was willing to sacrifice. We needed to arrive early, meet early, and conclude early. I needed as much time as possible at the mall to divert Mom's attention elsewhere while I got to where I needed to be.

Hair slicked back and a bib strategically placed over the stained portion of Andy's shirt, I smoothed my own hair back with nerve greased hands. I was beginning to feel a tad nauseous and wanted this to be over with as soon as possible.

Reverend Hall was waiting for us in the church sanctuary, which allowed me a clear view of the old and timely architecture of Grace Presbyterian. It was beautiful. The smell of a rich wood polish emanated the air. I could just hear history speaking to me from these two hundred year old walls.

The reverend was not exactly what I pictured, but he wasn't exactly a replica of Pastor Larry either. There was an uncanny resemblance in posture and verbal attitude, though. I decided it must be a "preacher thing."

We followed Reverend Hall and arranged ourselves comfortably in the high back velvet arm chairs that surrounded his desk. I almost wished the season was colder so maybe he would light the ornate fireplace located against a wall otherwise adorned with a massive book case.

This was the picture-perfect scene of all the old movies that I loved. So cozy, so warm, so Victorian.

As it was, we were served iced lemonade and offered delicate slices of lemon pound cake.

"Good morning, Elizabeth. I have so looked forward to meeting with you and your children."

First name basis already, huh? Mom had been busy.

"This must be the lovely Americka. So pleased to meet you. Your reputation precedes you." Uh-oh.

"My son raves about your singing and I understand you have made quite an impression on some old friends of mine."

I looked at my mother for any indication she understood what he was talking about. She looked as blank as I felt. *Who was his son? What reputation preceded me? Was this man of the cloth praising me? For what?*

"I would be honored to welcome you into the congregation here at Grace, but I want you to be comfortable with us as a church. Larry has a way with the young crowd and I am very proud of what he has done on his own at Sacred Sanctuary. I have lost several families to his charm, but the regulars still hang in there with me. It is almost as if son and father have a tag team ministry."

Of course. The resemblance became even more clear and I gawked, open mouth, at Reverend Hall.

My confusion must have been evident.

"Oh, I am sorry, Americka. Evidently I need to explain. My son decided to use his mother's maiden name when he started Sacred Sanctuary. To eliminate confusion. And I guess it worked!" Reverend Hall chuckled.

I could only stare at Reverend Hall as the truth struck me. He had no idea why my mother brought us here. *Had she not mentioned the cult activity at his son's church? Had she not made any kind of connection to Reverend Hall, conservative Presbyterian clergy, and Pastor Larry, renegade motorcycle minister?*

Wow.

My mother sputtered into her napkin as realization dawned on her. I really felt sorry for her just then. My mother, woman of nonjudgmental behavior, had been duped.

"Mrs. White tells me that you have had a healing influence on her Fiona, Americka. I am so happy Fiona has found joy in her life again. Her sister's untimely death has been extremely difficult. We feared we might lose Fiona as well. Thank you, Americka, for the friendship the two of you have formed. I have prayed for your family as well over the last months. It is truly a testament to our God that He brings individuals together in times of tragedy."

Mom wiped her lips and evidently had herself under control enough to join the so-far one-sided conversation.

"Your...your son is Pastor Larry of Sacred Sanctuary?"

Reverend Hall grinned a huge grin, eyes twinkling behind his oversized glasses. Yep. That was where Pastor Larry got those white teeth of his.

"I understand your confusion. Larry grew up in a rather stodgy church environment. His grandfather, my father, preached here at Grace for many years before I completed seminary and had the honor of taking his place. When Larry expressed interest in following in the family footsteps, I was concerned. My son has been a rebel from day one. But he maintained through high school and college that his convocation to be a spiritual leader was unquestionable. He just had, and has, a different way of presenting the message."

Reverend Hall cupped his chin in his hand as if reflecting on earlier days.

"His mother and I had to adjust our way of thinking a bit, but it all made sense. She understood more than I. Being a retired school teacher, she was more aware of the proper way to reach young folks. And I have to admit I enjoy the praise team every now and then. But it is, decidedly, for younger ears." Reverend Hall chuckled softly.

O-M-Goodness. My mother had arranged a counseling session for her wayward daughter with the father of the very minister she was trying to steer me clear of. This was priceless. If only it didn't put Mom in such an embarrassing position. With me. Not with the Reverend.

"But, enough chit-chat about my son. He is the reason you are here. And, as I understood correctly, our time is limited today. I do not want to make you late for the BIG SHOW, Americka."

As he rearranged a few papers on his desk, my mother shot another questioning look my way. She had to be totally flabbergasted by now. I knew I was.

A knock on the open door brought our attention to the newcomer and my lips nearly fell off my mouth at the sight of Holly and her mother, both looking immensely uncomfortable and totally not happy.

"I am sorry to interrupt, Reverend, but I simply must speak to you as soon as possible. Oh, I'm sorry. I didn't know you had an appointment this morning."

Holly's mother was literally wringing her hands while Holly only hung her head, thus avoiding any eye contact at all. From the slight glimpse at her face it was obvious she had been crying. This was not a social call. There was trouble in the Woods family and it must be serious enough to warrant a visit to the family minister.

"Yes, Mrs. Woods, Holly, I am actually in conference right now. Maybe you could come back later this afternoon? When I finish here, I actually have another engagement to attend. If this is of extreme importance of course I will make time for you before I go."

Holly sniffled in response and Mrs. Woods looked panicked.

"It is not necessarily life or death, Reverend, but we really need your council. Holly has found herself in a bit of a situation. I think your guidance would be most helpful."

"Reverend Hall, this appears to be of more urgency than our scheduled appointment. Why don't you attend to this matter and I will call to schedule a more convenient date next week?" Mom didn't even wait for a reply, but bounced Andy with her into an upright position and handed me the diaper bag.

"Yes, thank you, Elizabeth. It was a pleasure to meet the rest of your family and we will talk next week. Please join us tomorrow for Sunday service. We have a nice surprise for the congregation tomorrow that you won't want to miss." Reverend Hall actually winked at me before adding, "Good luck today, Americka. Or should I say, break a leg?"

Mom buckled Andy in his car seat, climbed into the driver's side of the running Toyota, and just sat there, hands on the steering wheel, staring ahead.

"I don't know what to make of all of this, Americka. Nothing seems to make sense. It's like a giant puzzle to which pieces continue to be added."

I nodded my head in agreement, even though she wasn't looking in my direction. She didn't know the half of it.

"Parenting is difficult, Americka. Making the correct decisions for your children, keeping them safe, and offering sound advice…it's all so very, very challenging. Your father was so good at this kind of thing. I miss him so much."

And there were the tears. Not the hysterical out of control sobbing of the bereaved, but a silent mourning. I hated to see my mother cry. I hated to see anyone cry, but especially my mother.

"I say let's skip the mall lunch and go home for a cheese sandwich." Mom put the car in gear and started to back out of the parking spot.

"No!"

I am so glad we were not going any faster because at the sound of my voice Mom slammed on the brakes, jerking us forward and issuing an Andy hiccup from the backseat.

"What? Was there something behind me, Americka?"

As she looked furiously around her for an errant child or a wondering dog , I found my voice.

"We have to go to the mall. I have to sing."

29

THE MAIN EVENT

Probably due to the talent show attendance, parking at the mall was more limited than normal, so Mom let me out at the main entrance.

Neither one of us commented on my speaking. I knew it was the first for me to voluntarily talk to my mother, but I still wasn't certain if she was aware of this pinnacle event. It didn't really matter right now.

I was at the mall, looking for my friends, getting ready for this performance that I had deemed silly only a few weeks ago.

Funny how time changes one's outlook. Right now this talent show was all I wanted to do. The heck with Holly and her irrational thoughts. Possible further punishment for my non-crimes could wait. I was at the mall. And I was going to sing.

Raymond and Fiona were at the Book Barn even though it was a little earlier than we had planned to meet. As soon as the door chimes announced my arrival, Fiona was all over me, asking questions, patting down my hair, announcing the day's specials and offering me an iced coffee all in the same breath. Typical Fiona style.

As soon as I was disentangled from Fiona's whirlwind, Raymond came at me with no hesitation and wrapped me in the warmest, nicest hug I could ever imagine.

"I'm so glad you made it, Meri. We had no doubts, though. We knew it would happen."

I didn't want him to but Raymond released me and led me over to the huge, overstuffed couch where he picked up his guitar and started strumming the opening chords of our song.

"Let's run through it?" He asked and Fiona squealed in assent.

"Yes, let's do it." Fiona took my hand and looked me sternly in the eye. "Let's do this thing. Let's sing. Let's make your father and my Daphne proud."

And so it was. We sang. We sang so clearly and loudly that I was certain Dad and Daphne could hear us from their prime viewing area. And I could swear I heard them clapping from that distant seat in the sky.

I was nervous at first, but then I found my mother and Andy in the crowd and her smile put me at ease. It was going to be okay. My family was going to heal and we were going to be just fine.

With another glance toward the audience I also found Pastor Larry standing beside his own dad, both smiling and waving at the participants on the stage. I even found Mademoiselles' lovely face beaming in my direction. She was standing near Fiona's mother and father and clapping wildly at our introduction. The rush of performance swept over me and I just wanted to sing. The contest prize meant nothing to me. In fact, I couldn't even remember what the prize was. I was just psyched to be here with my friends, singing for my family.

And it was a good thing that my emotions were running so generously. Because we didn't win. Our song had reached someone, though. The words were not lost. And we were even asked to perform an encore. The taste of victory filled my hungry soul as if we had consumed a five course meal.

Which we practically did at the restaurant afterwards. I looked around the full table at the faces of these people who meant so much to me. Mom and Andy, Fiona and Raymond, with an empty chair between them to symbolize Daphne's presence (okay, so we weren't totally healed), Mr. and Mrs. White, Pastor Larry and his father, even Mademoiselle and Aunt Lydia. They were all here and they all agreed to hold hands around the table for the blessing.

My life had taken some kind of weird turn and I was glad. I was sorry Holly couldn't see this, but I don't think she would understand. Not yet. As life was proving, there was plenty of room for miracles at the hands of the father and son team of Hall and Hawkins.

As Reverend Hall blessed our meal and the presence of each of us, I quietly lifted my eyes to the sky. I just knew Dad was part of this celebration. I caught Fiona's eye and realized that we both were breaking the unspoken law of mindful prayer. We had our eyes open.

I also realized we were both wearing Burt's Bees champagne lip shimmer. In the distance I heard cinematic bombs bursting in air. I winked at Fiona and she winked back and indicated with a nod of her head to follow her after the "amen."

We excused ourselves and walked arm in arm to the restroom. The door barely came to a close behind us before Fiona and I, arms around one another, crumpled to the dusty floor in a fit of stupid giggles.

EPILOGUE

"I am really going to miss you, Meri." Fiona hugged me again, even harder this time. If she didn't end her goodbyes she was going to miss her flight and she wouldn't have to worry about missing me. She would be stuck right there with me while her summer study in Paris went on without her.

If I had learned anything about life after Dad's death, it was to expect the unexpected. When Mademoiselle announced she was going "home" for the summer and she was disappointed none of her high school students had applied for the summer exchange student program offered at a university near her parent's home, Mrs. White got busy. This would be a perfect opportunity for Fiona. A new start. Something she could do on her own, without Daphne.

It sounded scary at first, but Fiona began practicing her textbook French and agreed to give it a go.

I was happy for her. She deserved a chance to be her own person. And I couldn't wait to see what wild fashion trends she brought home.

"I will send you a postcard every day!" She said as her mother laughingly pulled us apart.

"No, you won't. You will be too busy chatting up the local Parisians," I told her. "Have fun, Fiona."

"Yes, Fi-Fi, have a blast. Americka and I will be here when you return. Pinky promise," Raymond told her. "And we will be ready to record the next number one praise hit in the country. So don't forget to keep those vocal chords warm."

"Okay, *Ray-Ray*. You take care of my Meri-ca. Don't let her get away," Fiona winked down at our clasped hands. If my mother had noticed the turn in my relationship with Raymond, she hadn't commented. But, as I looked up at Raymond's shaggy head, I just knew this was going to be a very interesting summer.

When I got back to my room that afternoon, my foot made contact with a pile of papers that peeked out from under my bed. Tidying had taken an unfortunate lesser priority lately and I knew my mother was going to address this issue before long. So, I bent to retrieve the miscellaneous mound of "stuff."

Sheet music, a worn school notebook, and my moleskin Bible. I smiled as I caressed the soft cover of this first gift from Sacred Sanctuary. Who would have thought this is where it would lead me?

While I carried the Bible to a more appropriate resting spot on my bedside table, a single piece of paper floated toward the floor. My list of mysteries.

1. Daphne's death
2. Fiona's mysterious emotional ailments
3. Raymond's romantic involvement with the White sisters
4. My inability to speak in the presence of a select group of individualities
5. Raymond's involvement in Daphne's death
6. How to escape the house for rehearsal and the talent show
7. Why my parents owned this beautiful Bible, but never went to church
8. Why Holly had it out for me

I think I had my answer to all these issues. I noticed I had drawn a line through number 3 due to irrelevance. But I knew that number 3 was anything but irrelevant. Number three was all about me.

Post-Traumatic Stress Syndrome (PTSD) is a term most commonly used in reference to the emotional effect that follows the severe conditions a soldier experiences in times of war. But an individual does not have to be exposed to military battle in order to experience PTSD. Any strong emotional trauma can trigger the ill effects of a post trauma. The syndrome portion of the definition is associated with the length of time that such symptoms continue. The effects of PTSD reach further than the psychological and physical maladies of the actual soldier in times of war-related incidents. Family members also suffer the extreme consequences of battle scars.

Unlike our fictional Meri, individuals with PTSD require more than prayer and family as treatment in recovery. For more information, visit one of these websites:

http://www.veteransfreefromptsd.org/
http://www.joyfulheartfoundation.org/
http://www.mayoclinic.org